In Search of Liberty

In Search of Liberty

Ruth Nulton Moore

Illustrated by James Converse

Resource *Publications*

An imprint of *Wipf and Stock Publishers*
199 West 8th Avenue • Eugene OR 97401

Resource Publications
A division of Wipf and Stock Publishers
199 W 8th Ave, Suite 3
Eugene, OR 97401

In Search of Liberty
By Moore, Ruth Nulton
Copyright©1983 Herald Press
ISBN: 1-59752-271-6
Publication date 6/21/2005
Previously published by Herald Press, 1983

TO CARL,
who gave me the idea for this story
with the gift of a 1794 penny;

TO STEVE,
who suggested the ending;

and

TO CHUCK,
who believes that happiness
must be shared.

So long as Faith and Freedom reigns ...
Life is worth living still.

Alfred Austin

JON

J ON REED'S father stepped closer to his son's hospital bed. He smiled at the fourteen-year-old boy who lay between the crisp white sheets. "How goes it, son?" he asked.

Jon glanced down at his crippled right leg and forced a smile that made his face feel tight. "Okay, Dad."

"Tomorrow it'll be all over, Jon," Mr. Reed said. "And if the operation is successful, Dr. Bannon thinks you'll be able to walk without your brace."

"That'll be great, Dad."

There was a long silence; neither the boy nor his father could think of any more to say. Then Mr. Reed drew a small square box from his pocket. Jon watched his father open the box and take out a large copper coin. Holding it between his thumb and forefinger along the rounded edge, he held the coin out for Jon to see.

"This is my good luck penny," Mr. Reed told his son. "It was given to me by my father when I was a boy, and I have been waiting for the right time to give it to you. I believe now's the time."

Jon opened his eyes wide and wriggled up in bed to get a

11

better look at the coin. When his father turned it toward the light, the copper shone like burnished gold. Engraved on one side was a woman's head with long flowing hair. Jon squinted to get a better look at the head. Across the shoulder was a thin pole with a funny little cap hanging on the end of it. Above the head was the word *Liberty* and at the bottom of the coin was the date, 1794.

"Wow, 1794!" Jon exclaimed.

His father handed him the coin. "It's your good luck penny now, son. You can do with it whatever you wish, but I know you'll want to keep it."

"I sure will," Jon said. He flipped the coin over to look at the other side. The words *One Cent* were engraved on the back, surrounded by two laurel branches. Circling the branches were the words *United States of America.*

"I never saw a penny this old before," Jon said excitedly.

"That's because it was one of the very first cent pieces minted in the United States," Mr. Reed told him.

Both Jon and his father shared the hobby of collecting old coins, and Jon had quite a collection of his own. He turned the penny over again. "Pennies were a lot bigger in 1794 than they are now," he observed. "But what's the lady's head supposed to represent, and what kind of funny little cap is that on the stick across her shoulder?"

"The head represents Liberty. It's called the Liberty head," said Mr. Reed. "The pole across the left shoulder is topped with the conical cap Roman slaves wore when they became free men. The coin is called a Liberty Cap cent. It tells a story, son, doesn't it?"

"What do you mean, Dad? What story?" asked Jon.

"Well," Mr. Reed explained, sitting on the edge of Jon's bed, "the Liberty Cap cent was minted in Philadelphia during the French Revolution. In France, at that time, the peasants adopted the conical cap as a symbol of liberty and carried their caps on poles across their shoulders to protest tyranny and to proclaim their freedom."

"Wow," Jon said again, "this coin was minted during the French Revolution! That's neat, Dad." Then a puzzled frown wrinkled his brow. "But why did you call it your good luck penny?"

"Because it's the name my grandfather said his father called the penny when it was given to him. It seems that this old cent piece has brought good luck to all those who have possessed it. At least that's what my father told me," Mr. Reed replied. "It's been in the family a good many years, son. As far back as your great-great-grandfather James Reed. The story goes that a Nez Percé Indian gave the penny to James Reed for saving his life."

"An Indian gave this penny to my great-great-grandfather!" exclaimed Jon. "How did he save the Indian's life?"

Mr. Reed shook his head. "I don't know the details of the story, Jon. All I know is that was how the penny got into our family."

Jon looked down at the old coin, then up at his father again. "Do you really think it brings good luck, Dad?"

Mr. Reed cocked his head with a grin. "I sure hope so, Jon. That's why I'm giving it to you now."

At that moment the nurse came into the room. Mr. Reed reached for his coat and hat. "I guess it's time to say good night, Jon. Shall we say a prayer together before I go?"

Jon nodded and held tightly to his father's hand as Mr. Reed asked God's blessing on his son. Then he bent over to kiss Jon on the forehead. "Good night, son. Your mother and I will be here tomorrow—after the operation."

Jon felt a lump rise in his throat as he waved good-bye to

13

his father. Then Miss Karcher handed him a pill and a glass of water. "To make you sleep," she said. "Before you know it, Jon, it'll be all over and your leg will be feeling just fine."

"I hope so," he said in a choked voice.

Miss Karcher turned off his light and swished efficiently out of the room. A stab of fear pierced Jon as he lay there alone. He had never had an operation before. He wondered what it would be like. He knew that he would be asleep during the actual operation and not feel a thing, but what if he didn't wake up after the operation was over? And when he did wake up, would there be terrible pain?

The dark hospital walls seemed to close in on him, and he thought that any minute he would have to call out for the nurse. Then he remembered that he had promised Dad he would be brave. Besides, he was too old to call out like a little kid.

"I won't think about the old operation," he told himself, swallowing the lump in his throat. "Instead, I'll think about my good luck penny."

He turned on the night light above his bed and opened his fingers to look down at the penny. He bent his head to examine it closely. There was a scratch mark on the head of Liberty that he hadn't noticed before. It was just under the chin and ran across the hair to the liberty cap. He wondered how such a long scratch mark had got there.

Well, the penny was very old, he mused, and must have passed through many hands before it was given to his great-great-grandfather. Why, George Washington was president of the United States in 1794 when this penny was minted. Besides collecting old coins, Jon was an American history buff and knew his presidents well.

Suddenly he was feeling very drowsy. He lay back on his pillow and blinked down at the penny. He wondered how

14

many other hands had held it the way he was holding it. The thought intrigued him.

Were there others, as frightened as he was now, who had held this penny for comfort? His fingers curled around the copper coin. What kind of people were they, he wondered. Was one of them a boy like himself?

He sighed deeply, and his eyelids flickered shut. How many other hands . . . Who were they. . . .

THE SWEEP

1

THE SWEEP squirmed up the long flue with his knees and elbows, a human fly clinging to the inside of the chimney. Wielding his brush and scraper, the tools of his trade, he sent a shower of soot cascading down to the blanket below. He wriggled upward again, slowly and carefully, fighting down the panic that tightened his throat. He knew all too well that any false movement might send him plummeting downward to the stone hearth.

Aye, many a pore sweep wuz crippled or killed that way, he thought ruefully. *An' bein' caught in a tight spot in th' bloomin' flue an' not bein' able t'wiggle out—well that meant th' end fer sure.*

The sweep lifted the edge of his stocking cap and looking upward, he glimpsed a glimmer of light. Squirming toward it, he emerged at last from the top of the chimney. He coughed and spat the chimney's soot on the roof slates; then like a crow perched on its high nest, he looked out over the city through watery eyes.

He always liked this moment, hanging at the top of the chimney where he could look over the sea of rooftops to the ships on the river. It made him feel as free as a bird, and for a glorious moment he forgot that he was one of Mr. O'Malley's apprentices who cleaned out the soot-filled chimneys of Philadelphia.

The sudden banging of the poker against the andirons broke through his brief reverie and sent him corkscrewing down the chimney at his master's bidding. An angry Mr. O'Malley coughed and cursed as the sweep gathered the pile of soot in the old blanket and slung it over his skinny shoulders, sending a dark cloud over the big man. Gathering the brushes and scrapers, Mr. O'Malley gave the boy a kick that sent him staggering out into the street with his heavy load while he, the master, remained behind for his pay.

The sweep dreaded the long walk with his sooty bundle down crowded Chestnut Street. It made him feel like an outcast when people made faces and shied away from him. Well-dressed ladies would gather together their skirts and move to the other side of the walk with distaste. Sometimes tradesmen would shout angry threats if he came near their wares. Nobody had anything to do with a grimy chimney sweep, bent over like a black gnome with his heavy sack.

Aye, ye dirty sweep, nobody loves ye, that's a fact, he thought as he trudged along. He hadn't been a sweep long and his sore elbows and knees hadn't calloused up yet. Some of the older sweeps were proud of their black callouses and scabs. It was a mark that they had matured in their trade. But most of them coughed up blood all the time which meant that they hadn't long to work.

20

He didn't intend to be working long either. He'd not be a sweep all his life, he vowed. He passed the Statehouse with its tall brick tower and caught a glimpse of the broad river at the street's end. He looked longingly at the sloops and schooners tied to the docks. *Ah-h, he'd not be a bloomin' sweep all his life.*

He didn't remember his mother. They told him she had died when he was born. The only home he knew was the foundling home and then the almshouse. He was told by the overseer of the poor that his name was Jeremy, but nobody knew who his father was or what had become of him. When he was old enough to work, Jeremy was apprenticed to Mr. O'Malley, who was supposed to be a master bricklayer, but nobody cared that the boy was not learning a proper trade as his papers said. Aye, who cared for the sweep who didn't even know his last name?

He had often wondered what his surname was, and he was determined that when he became of age, he'd give himself a proper-sounding one. He tried Abbott and Johnson and Grey and other names, trying to find one that would go with Jeremy. One time when he was caught sounding the names aloud by the older boys, they laughed at him and said, "Ye'll niver be called anything but Sweep, Half Pint, as long as ye lives. So wot ye want another name fer?"

He lived in a shed with the other sweeps behind Mr. O'Malley's house which was at the end of an alley near the waterfront. Often at night he would lie awake on his straw pallet, listening to the ships' bells and wondering how he could escape his miserable existence.

He had heard of runaways hiding out in the city or escaping across the river to the New Jersey side. But most of them were dragged back to their masters and flogged within a

21

breath of their lives. No, he decided, when he found a chance to escape, he'd head for the docks. There was always a ship or two leaving Philadelphia for a distant city along the Atlantic coast, and once a ship was on its way down the river, nobody would be able to drag him back to Mr. O'Malley's.

The sweep was so deep in his miserable thoughts that at first he didn't notice a group of street boys straggling along behind him. But when he heard a snicker and knew they were there, his heart gave a thump and he quickly threaded his way down a narrow side street, hoping to lose them.

He felt panic rise up inside him when he heard them following. One of the boys reached down for a loose cobblestone, and a moment later the sweep felt a sharp pain in his left shoulder. He staggered under the blow of it.

The pain sent anger rising up inside him and he swung around, shouting curses. Another boy dashed up and spat in his dirty face. "Ho, ye stinkin' soot devil, git off th' street and let us pass."

"Ho, stinkin' soot devil! Ho, stinkin' soot devil!" the other three chanted.

The sweep knew he should ignore them and keep trudging on down the street. Mr. O'Malley had told him this often enough. But what little pride that was left in him made him bristle at their taunts, and before he realized what he was doing, he stopped abruptly and swung his heavy load at them.

The blanket tore apart and grimy soot showered over the four. While they coughed and sputtered, the sweep broke loose and ran in the direction of Mr. O'Malley's. But before he could reach his shed, the four caught up with him and surrounded him. Their faces were as grimy as his, and he could see the anger in the whites of their eyes.

22

He fought back as well as he could, but the merciless fists rained down on his head and shoulders. When he fell to the cobblestones and didn't move, they let up on their blows and wandered on down the street, laughing and hooting and calling him vile names.

He moaned and rolled over on his back. How long he lay there in a half daze he didn't know. But when his vision cleared, he managed to crawl to a sitting position on a doorstep. It was then that he felt the hand on his shoulder and looked up at the mistress of the house who had come out to see what all the commotion was.

"Are thee badly hurt?" she asked.

He looked up at her through puffy eyes. She had a kind face and wore the long gray dress and round white cap of a Quaker lady. Bending over him, she resembled a gentle dove, he thought.

"Thee are a chimney sweep, are thee not?" she added quickly. Then without waiting for an answer, she hurried back into the house and appeared moments later with a cup of cold water.

The sweep gulped down the water and felt much better.

"Ah-h, thank ye. I best be goin'," he said as he lifted himself up by the help of the gatepost.

But before he left, the gentle woman pressed a coin into his sooty hand. " 'Tis not much, but it just came new from the mint," she told him. "A brand new penny brings good luck, they say. Be on thy way now, Sweep, and may God bless thee."

The boy staggered on down the street. Without realizing it, he had turned from the direction of Mr. O'Malley's and was heading toward the river where the big ships lay at anchor.

He paused before crossing Front Street and looked

around warily to see if anyone was following. Then like a witless imp he skittered on to Water Street where the smells of the waterfront greeted him—fishy, spicy, tarry—the odors of strange cargoes from faraway ports.

He hurried along the busy docks, past brigs and schooners and clippers that thrust their bowsprits toward the shops and taverns that lined the street. He was passing a sailors' tavern when the door was flung open and he found himself in a tangle of a dozen brown-faced men with rings in their ears and long tarred pigtails. It was too late to run, for they had already surrounded him.

"Well, wot have we here?" roared their spokesman.

The sweep hung his head and tried to hide his soot-streaked face and grimy sores.

"Methinks 'tis a bloody sweep," another sailor piped up, backing off from the frightened boy. "He could stand a wee bit o' dunkin' in the drink," he added, holding his nose.

The sweep's heart pounded. He didn't know how to swim, and if they threw him into the river, he'd be a goner for sure.

"Aye, let's try to git th' soot devil lily-white," laughed another sailor, pressing closer.

They grabbed at his filthy clothes and were about to push him into the river when a voice boomed out from the rear of the group. "Let th' pore little sot go, mates, an' may th' good Lord have mercy on his black soul."

With roars of laughter, the sailors let go of him and moved off down the street in a rolling gait. Letting out his breath with relief, the sweep leaped to the other side of the street and slid down behind the piling of a dock. Exhausted, he leaned his aching head on his knees. "Ah-h, ye got no-body in th' world wot loves ye, ye stinkin' soot devil," he moaned.

After a few minutes of self-pity, he lifted his eyes and blinked at the schooner tied by the dock in front of him. He stared at the tall masts, the spiderweb of rigging, the furled sails. He had never been so close to a ship before.

He wiped his bleeding nose with the back of his grimy hand and discovered that he was still clutching the coin the Quaker lady had given him. He opened his fingers and looked down at it. It was a brand-new shiny copper penny with the year 1794 stamped on it. When she had dropped it into his hand, the gentle lady had said that a brand-new penny brought good luck. Aye, he would need plenty of that!

A tear slid down his cheek and he wiped it away with a swipe of his black fingers. It was the first time anyone had ever spoken a kind word to him, and a strange new emotion he had never felt before rose up inside him.

Roughly he rubbed his cheek dry and kept staring at the shiny new coin. Would it really bring him good fortune? he wondered. Then captured by the old dream, he looked up again at the schooner before him.

2

THE SWEEP hid behind the piling until nightfall. Behind him now the city glowed with candlelight and hummed with the echoes from noisy taverns along Water Street. Before him was the dark river and silence.

The schooner at the end of the dock loomed over him like a black creature, its ship's lantern winking at him like a friendly eye. In its dim light he could read her name: *Marianne*.

From his hiding place that afternoon he had overheard a sailor say that the *Marianne* would be setting sail in the morning with a cargo of cotton goods for Charleston. The sweep didn't know where Charleston was, but it didn't matter. Home to him could be any place, just so it was miles away from Philadelphia chimneys and Mr. O'Malley.

The sweep kept his eyes on the dock, and when he was

sure no one was around, he eased up from the piling and crept along the pier's edge until he reached the gangplank of the *Marianne*. For once he was glad for his sooty appearance which let him blend into the dark night. He hesitated before the gangplank for a breathless moment, then scrambled aboard the schooner like an agile monkey.

Reaching the deck, he looked furtively around him. The ship seemed empty. The crew must all be ashore, he reasoned, celebrating their last night in port.

He took off his shoes and stuffing them into his shirt, he scooted across the deck to an open hatch. As he peered through it, the most delectable smell rose up to fill his nostrils. Chowder! The cook must have made fish chowder for supper, and the tantalizing smell still lingered in the galley.

The sweep's gaze swept the empty deck again before he scooted down the steep galley steps. By the light of a lantern swinging from the rafters, he spied a big kettle on the stove and discovered that there was some chowder left at the bottom of it. Ravenously he scooped out the chunks of fish and potatoes, stuffing them into his mouth with his fingers. He bent over the still warm kettle and scraped the bottom clean. Never in his life had he had so much good food, and he felt almost giddy as he made his way up the galley steps.

He had just crept onto the deck when he heard a footfall on the gangplank. Looking wildly about him, he saw to the starboard two lifeboats. Like a frightened creature, he skittered across the deck and slid into one of the boats. It was big and roomy and had a heavy tarpaulin over it to keep him out of sight.

He held his breath and lay rigid until the footsteps echoed away below deck. Then, relaxing, he curled up on the bottom of the dory, and resting his head on a coil of rope, he dropped off into a deep and peaceful sleep.

How long he had slept, he had no idea. It was a strange rocking motion that awoke him. He sat up stiffly and peered out from the edge of the tarpaulin. The bright morning light almost blinded him, and he had to blink several times before he could look up at the white sails billowing out in a stiff breeze. The *Marianne* was on her way to Charleston!

He unfolded his cramped legs and cautiously slid out of the lifeboat to drop down between it and the lee rail of the ship. He filled his lungs with tangy sea air which made him feel suddenly lightheaded. Clutching the rail, he looked around him, but the dock and the waterfront and the red-brick chimneys of Philadelphia were gone. All he could see on the empty far horizon was the gray sky.

He grasped the rail tighter. Wherever he looked were the limitless stretches of leaden water. *Ah-h, without even knowin' it, ye sailed down th' river, out through th' bay, and on t' th' Atlantic Ocean,* he told himself with a crooked grin. Well, he wasn't sad at having missed saying good-bye to Philadelphia and her dirty chimneys, that was certain.

A sudden tilt of the deck as the prow cut through the waves and the ship heeled gracefully to the wind sent his head reeling again. Presently he felt a rush of sickness at the lift and roll of the ship, and after he had hung over the rail for what seemed an eternity, he staggered back into the lifeboat.

Exhausted from his seasickness, he napped off and on in the semidarkness, vaguely aware of the ship's bell and the bosun's whistle. During the dogwatch in the late afternoon, he was awakened by the sound of voices near the lifeboats. Alert now, the sweep raised his head and listened.

"We're in for a bad blow," said one voice.

"Aye, we are by the looks of the barometer," replied the

other. "I hope it holds off till we get past Cape Hatteras. The sea's rough enough there in balmy weather." The voices drifted off and there was silence again.

The sweep wondered what it would be like to be on the ocean during a storm. Well, it didn't matter. He had a snug berth in the lifeboat, with a tarpaulin over his head to keep off the rain. His seasickness had left him, and he was anxious for night to come when he could get out of his cramped quarters and move about the deck. The memory of the tasty chowder the night before made his mouth water, and he decided that as soon as the cook bedded down for the night, he'd head for the galley.

The boy dozed off again, and when he awoke the next time, it was so dark that he couldn't see his hand in front of him. He lifted the tarpaulin and peered out at the deck. It seemed to be empty except for dim lantern light in the foredeck where a group of sailors sat, playing cards and spinning yarns. If he kept to the shadows, the sweep thought, they wouldn't see him slip across the deck to the galley.

He climbed out of the lifeboat and crept from shadow to shadow. By now he was so hungry that he could smell the chowder before he reached the hatch. Perhaps he could find a sea biscuit to go with it and some good strong tea. *Aye, ye'll soon be dinin' on a meal fit fer a king,* he told himself with a crooked grin.

As before, he carefully surveyed the galley before he climbed through the hatch. The lantern swinging from the rafters had been trimmed down to a lower light which, the sweep thought, was a good sign that the cook had cleaned up and gone to his bunk.

The boy made straight for the chowder kettle. He had just succeeded in scooping up his first mouthful of fish and potatoes when he heard a cry and swung around to see a pair of wide flopping pants descending the galley steps.

The boy leaped away from the kettle. He ducked this way and that, trying to make a run for it, but the bulky form in front of the galley steps blocked his way and a hand like an iron vise reached out and clamped around his skinny shoulder.

"Ha, so ye be the little thief wot likes me chowder!" the cook's voice rang out. "A wee bit o' varmint stowed away on this ship, be ye?"

The sweep recoiled instinctively, then reached into his pocket and drew out his penny. Holding it up for the cook to see, he ventured in a desperate voice, "How's fer a copper fer some chowder?"

The angry cook grabbed his shoulders with both hands and shook him like a dustrag. The penny flew out of the boy's hand, rang harshly against the edge of the kettle, then spun like a top on the floor by his feet.

"A copper fer me chowder, eh?" The cook's big round face was as red as raw beefsteak. "It's to th' captain ye'll be goin', me hearty. Now come along with ye."

The sweep shook himself loose just long enough to retrieve his penny. In an instant the big hand was on him again, jerking him upright. Grabbing the boy's ear tightly between thumb and forefinger, the cook marched him up the galley steps and across the deck to the captain's quarters in the aft.

3

AH-H—YE BLOOMIN' sweep, ye landed yerself into a fine kettle o' stew this time, the boy told himself as he peered around the dark brig deep in the hold of the ship. Well, he had a sure passage to Charleston, he thought, reflecting his fate, but what would happen to him when the *Marianne* got into port? Would it be jail and then slaving for another master? Or, worse yet, would the captain send him back to Philadelphia to the wrath of Mr. O'Malley? Aye, he really had landed himself into a fine kettle of stew!

He lay back on a pile of filthy straw and tried to sleep, but the creaking of the ship's timbers and the pounding of waves against its sides kept him awake. The schooner tossed and groaned as it pitched to and fro, rocking him from one side of the straw pallet to the other.

The pitch-black hold made the storm seem all the more

frightening. The sweep felt as if he were in a deep, dark pit with everything closing in, squeezing the life out of him. He had had that same panicky feeling every time he had started up a chimney.

Suddenly the ship plunged down, down into the trough of a wave, and the boy's stomach plunged with it. He thought they would never come up again, that they would be sucked into the very bowels of the ocean. But with a terrible shudder and groan the schooner began to climb out of the wave. There was a brief, breathless calm until the ship went down again in another horrible glide into the trough of another wave.

The boy held his arms tightly around his stomach and crouched over the pile of straw. Above his retching, he tried to shut out the sounds of the raging storm. This was the end, he thought. Soon all his worries would be over. Imagine a filthy chimney sweep like himself dying in the water! The thought almost made him grin.

He supposed that people prayed before they died, that they asked God to forgive their sins and to have mercy on their souls. He wondered if his mother had prayed before she died.

He clasped his grimy hands together, and as the storm roared around him, he cried out to a God he only vaguely knew. "If ye'll listen t' this pore lil' sweep, Sir, I mean t' tell ye I'm sorry fer wot sins I done, and if ye can have mercy on me black, miserable soul, I'd thank ye kindly."

With that a wave pounded so hard against the timbers that the sweep thought for sure the ocean would break through. He crouched farther down in the straw as the schooner shuddered and groaned. He had his hands over his ears and his eyes were squeezed so tightly shut that he did not hear the key turning in the lock of the brig door nor did he see the wavering trail of light coming toward him. Not until he felt something grab his arm did his eyes fly open.

His mouth gaping with wonder, he glimpsed the door of the brig swinging open and shut with the roll of the ship. In the light of a smoky lantern, he blinked at the distorted face bending over his—at the sharp black eyes gleaming over a long pointed nose, at the wide mouth showing its teeth.

At first he thought it was the devil, himself, come to fetch him, but when a voice spoke to him, it sounded human enough. "Come with me, boy. Hurry!"

Before he moved an inch he gasped, "Who—who be ye?"

"The first mate, Mister Roberts," the voice replied. "Now follow me."

Eager to escape his foul prison, the sweep scrambled after the first mate. As they staggered through the hold to the roll and pitch of the schooner, the sweep glanced fearfully at the wooden ribs above him. With each blow from the sea, he hoped that the beams would hold.

Mister Roberts led the way through the cargo to a pile of massive rocks that served as ballast at the stern end of the hold. He grabbed the sweep's collar and pulled him to a halt before the rocks. "There's a leak back there, lad, and the shifted ballast prevents the ship's carpenter from getting to it to repair it."

The sweep looked down and noticed a widening stream of water seeping out from under the rocks. Mister Roberts pushed him down to his knees. "See that space between the rocks where they shifted?"

The boy peered through the narrow opening.

"Do you think you can squeeze through, lad, and caulk the leak? It must be done at once before it gets too big to repair."

Before the boy could answer, a voice replied out of the

darkness, "Aye, sir, 'e looks skinny enough t' git th' rope through, and wot with 'im bein' a sweep an' all, I vow 'e knows how t' git past tight spots."

The sweep twisted his head. Behind them was the ship's carpenter who held out a tar bucket and a bristly black brush. "If ye can wiggle through that opening, sweep, I'll hand th' bucket and brush through t' ye and tell ye how t' mend th' leak."

The sweep nodded and pulled off his tattered coat and leather breeches. He tied the rope the first mate handed him around his narrow waist and smoothing his stocking cap down over his head as he did each time he went up a chimney, he started through the narrow space between the fallen rocks.

Ah-h, ye are a crazy one, squirmin' through an openin' no bigger than a bent flue and wi' a pile o' rocks waitin' t' come down on ye any minute, he thought as he corkscrewed his way into the opening. *But wot other choice has ye? It's either this or back t' th' bloody brig.*

He held his breath as the ship tossed and the timbers creaked. At one time he thought he heard the grating sound of a rock slipping, but with pounding heart he kept wriggling through the jagged opening.

By the light of the lanterns behind him, he could now see the timbers of the ship behind the ballast and the deep crack where sea water was seeping through. He had almost reached the timbers when the grating sound became louder, and his heart skipped a beat as a rock above his head slid halfway across the opening, narrowing it to almost half its size.

Now wot? he thought. He reached up and felt around the opening. Maybe, just maybe, if he imagined himself no wider than the rope around his waist, he could make it

34

through. Holding his breath, he drew in his stomach until it ached and started squirming around the corner of the rock. First his arms went through the hole, next his head, and now slanting his shoulders sidewise, straining downward with his hips until the sharp edge of rock gouged him and he almost cried out, the rest of his skinny body slipped through. He landed on the ship boards in a puddle of cold seawater and lay there for a long moment, gasping for breath.

At the tug of the rope around his waist, the sweep sat up and stared at the deep crack in the ship's wooden side.

"Look sharp, boy. We'll be handing in the tar and brush," Mister Roberts called through the rocks.

The sweep drew in the rope around his waist. On the other end was the brush and the tar bucket. With his cap he mopped the crack in the wood as dry as he could, and following the ship carpenter's instructions, he caulked the opening in the boards with a thick layer of tar. He waited until the tar hardened and he was sure that no more seawater seeped through the crack; then he gave the rope a tug and started back through the ballast.

"Well done, lad," Mister Roberts said when the sweep tore himself out of the opening. "Now get into your clothes and come up on deck with me. We need every hand we can get to help us through this storm."

4

THE DARK shadows on the deck were turning gray, and there was a pale glow along the rim of the sea to the east. The schooner still tossed, but the waves were no longer pounding it. The gray ocean heaved gently now as if it were catching its breath after last night's fury.

The crew were busy climbing the ratlines to the yards, and one by one the sails unfurled and caught the wind. The schooner heeled gracefully and picked up speed. The sweep, huddled against the bulwarks, watched the snapping billow of spreading canvas.

On the quarterdeck Mister Roberts stopped to talk with the helmsman, haunched wearily over the wheel. A stiff sea breeze carried their words across the deck to the sweep.

"We're clear of Hatteras now, Mister Wells. It should be smoother sailing."

"Aye, sir," the helmsman replied. "If the wind holds, we should be in Charleston tomorrow."

The sweep, shivering in the cold morning air, plunged his hands into his pockets. His fingers touched the penny and he drew it out to look at it again. A long scratch mark now marred its smooth surface from where it had bounced off the iron kettle in the galley the night before. But the coin still shone new, like burnished gold, as the boy tilted it in his hand.

His fingers closed around it stiffly when he heard Mister Roberts' footsteps coming down the deck in his direction. "Ho, lad," the first mate called briskly, "the captain wants a word with you. Follow me."

Still clutching his coin, the sweep rose to his feet, every muscle in his thin body aching. Like a small bedraggled monkey, he hobbled after the mate to the cabin in the aft.

A lantern still burned brightly through the cabin windows. With the slow roll of the schooner, its light threw long, wavering shadows across the polished walls and ceiling beams. It dropped a pool of light on the heavyset man who sat in the middle of the cabin, drumming his fingers on a tabletop. Before the captain stood Mister Roberts, with the sweep by his side, visually nervous.

The captain's stern face was gray after the sleepless night of the storm. He looked up through heavy dark brows at the grimy imp before him.

"What is your name, sweep?" he barked.

"Jeremy," the boy replied in a hoarse whisper.

The captain cleared his throat with a little cough. "Well, Jeremy, you know that being caught as a stowaway has grave consequences. However, Mister Roberts here tells me that you did us a good turn last night by mending a leak in the hold."

"Aye, sir," the sweep replied meekly.

The captain rose and walked over to the little windows along the back of the cabin. He pushed the curtain aside and looked out at the ocean. "Why do you want to go to Charleston, lad? Are you running away from your master?"

When the sweep didn't reply, the captain said sternly, "I should send you right back to Philadelphia, you know. You broke the law, lad, by breaking your bond and leaving your rightful master."

The sweep nodded woefully and looked down at his sooty shoes.

The captain turned back to the table and drew in an impatient breath. "Do you have any relatives that you know of?"

The sweep shook his head.

The captain sat down and studied his hands fanned out upon the table. "Well, there is an almshouse in Charleston that we can take you to. They'll see that you are bound out to another master who will teach you a trade."

The sweep's head jerked up quickly. Forgetting his fear of the captain, he cried out, "No, no!" Then in a rush of words he begged, "Sir, I'd like t' stay right here on this ship, if it please ye."

"Stay here?" roared the captain incredulously. "A chimney sweep on the *Marianne!*"

The boy nodded and swallowed hard.

"Sir," Mister Roberts spoke up, "I have seen this lad in the storm last night. A tough little scrapper he was, squirming through the ballast, then helping the men on deck with the lines. I think with some sound instruction we can make a worthy seaman out of him."

The captain frowned at the boy, but now the sweep returned his look with a steady gaze. No longer was he cowering before the captain. Mister Roberts' words had put courage into his scrawny bones. "Ye'll not be regrettin' takin' me on, sir," he answered boldly. "I fancies th' sea, I does."

The captain's dark brows arched with surprise. "You fancy the sea after that blow last night?"

"Aye, sir," the sweep replied with a crooked grin.

The captain threw back his head and laughed. "A peppery scamp you are!" Turning to his first mate, he said, "You say this lad was a tough little scrapper in the storm last night. Well, I reckon that's what this ship needs—a tough little scrapper. If you will be responsible for making him into a worthy cabin boy, Mister Roberts, we'll give him a try."

Early the next morning the *Marianne* entered the bay at Charleston. The sun, a red disk coming up out of the dark ocean, promised a bright, warm day. The bay was as gray and as tranquil as the back of a gull. The schooner glided evenly through its waters and up a broad river to the gracious old city.

The sweep and the first mate stood along the lee rail and watched the big stately houses glide by along the riverbank.

"If you're going to be a member of this crew, Jeremy, you'll have to look like a sailor," Mister Roberts said. "First thing we'll do when we get leave is to fit you out with proper clothes."

"Aye, sir, it'll be a blessin' gettin' rid o' these stinkin' rags," the sweep replied.

"By the way, Jeremy, what is your last name?" asked Mister Roberts.

The sweep looked down at his black-stained hands and didn't reply.

"You don't know?" asked the first mate.

The sweep shook his head miserably. He hesitated an instant; then looking up at the tall man by his side, he said, "Would ye mind, sir, if I borrow yer name?"

A surprised look came upon the first mate's face. "Why—why I guess not, lad."

"Then it be Roberts," the sweep said, sounding his new name slowly and with pride. "That's wot I'll call meself from now on, sir. Jeremy Roberts."

The first mate laughed and moved closer to the boy. "Jeremy Roberts it is, then," he agreed.

As the *Marianne* drifted in toward the docks, Jeremy Roberts reached into his jacket pocket and his hand closed around the penny. The Quaker lady in Philadelphia had said that a brand-new penny brought good luck. And it had. He'd give it a name, too, he decided. From now on he'd call it his good luck penny.

The sweep grinned his crooked grin as he looked at the beautiful city before him. *Aye, he wuz comin' into Charleston in fine style, he wuz. He had a new last name an' a lucky copper. Wot more could a bloomin' sweep want than that!*

JOSHUA

THE LEVEE was a busy place that warm July morning of 1808. The *Magnolia Belle* had just sailed up the Mississippi River, and as soon as she was docked, Mr. John Carver's slaves began loading the hold with bales of cotton.

The captain stood by the rail, idly watching the loading. He stiffened when he saw the overseer flick his bullwhip over the back of a slave to get him to work faster. "Slavery is an ugly business," the captain remarked to his first mate.

"Aye, sir, and Mr. Carver's overseer is one of the worst," the first mate replied.

Captain Jeremy Roberts looked over the heads of the slaves and across the levee to the big house that crowned the green lawn above the riverbank. Stately oaks, draped with flowing gray moss, lined the long drive leading up to it. With its gleaming white pillars and wide verandas it was a beautiful mansion. The captain had never been in it nor had he ever met its owner. Jeremy Roberts was the captain of a riverboat that stopped for Mr. Carver's cotton, and he dealt only with the overseer.

The captain left the rail and walked down the gangplank.

43

While the cotton was being loaded, he'd stretch his legs a bit. The willows overhanging the river promised cool shade, so he headed in their direction.

A path through the trees took him away from the grunts of the slaves and the sharp commands of the overseer. Beyond the willows stretched acres and acres of cotton fields, and on the other side of the riverbank rolled the big Mississippi.

Captain Roberts loved the broad, meandering river. He loved its rapid currents and quiet coves. It was like a living thing, this river—like a pulsing artery flowing through the heartland of America. He knew the first time he laid eyes on the Mississippi that he had found his destiny at last. He would be a captain on one of her riverboats.

A sound nearby broke through his reverie and caused him to pause and listen. There it was again, a choking, sobbing sound as if somebody were crying his heart out. It seemed to come from the riverbank, from behind that big willow just ahead.

Captain Roberts made his way to the tree and glimpsed a curly black head leaning against the trunk, facing downriver. The boy wore an old, worn shirt that was several sizes too big for him. The cuffs were rolled back almost to his elbows. He was about eleven years of age, the captain judged, but one couldn't be sure because the boy was so skinny. His loud sobs prevented him from hearing the man's approach, and it was not until Captain Roberts was standing by his side that the boy first noticed him. He leaped from the tree like a frightened rabbit and would have scampered away if the captain had not reached out and held him by the arm.

"Avast there, lad," Captain Roberts said, using a nautical term he had learned from a first mate he had known long ago and whose surname he had taken. "I won't hurt you,

44

boy. Now tell Captain Roberts what ails you. Do you have a bellyache? Were you whipped by your master?"

The captain's kind voice seemed to put the boy at ease. The look of fear on the black, crumpled face slowly vanished, and the boy wiped the tears off his cheek with the back of his hand. He shook his head twice in answer to the captain's questions.

"Well, then, what is the matter?" Captain Roberts persisted. "I can't think of much worse than a bellyache or being whipped."

The boy didn't answer but turned away and stared sorrowfully downriver.

"You're not thinking of running away, lad, are you?" asked the captain.

This time he was answered by a voice coming through the trees that separated the cotton fields. "Oh no, sir. He ain't fixin' to run away."

Captain Roberts swung around to see a tall black field hand coming toward them. "He's stayin' right here on Massa Carver's plantation where he belong," the man said. "Now come along, Joshua. Ain't no time to be cryin'. There's work for you to do, and Massa Carver'll be mad as a wet rooster if he sees you mopin' around like this."

The boy was about to follow the man back to the cotton fields when Captain Roberts stepped quickly in front of the field hand and demanded, "Tell me what ails the boy."

For a moment the tall, black man frowned down at the short riverboat captain; then he, too, gazed sorrowfully at the river. "His ma and daddy was sold downriver this mornin', sir, but the slave trader didn't want no boy, so Joshua here was separated from them. Probably won't never see them again."

At these words, the boy's mouth twisted and he tried to

45

choke back the sobs. The field hand gave his shoulders a little shake. "Now, Joshua, you be stayin' with me and Rebecca in our cabin. You hear? You ain't s'posed to mind if your ma and daddy is sold away from you. It happen all the time, boy."

Captain Robert's heart gave a lurch, and he felt a great sadness well up inside him. It may happen all the time, but how could you stop the tears from coming when the parents you loved so much were snatched away from you? It was as hurtful as sudden death.

The image of a dirty chimney sweep whom nobody loved flashed through the captain's mind. He knew how hard life was without parents to love you and to care for you. His hand went automatically into the pocket of his greatcoat, and his fingers curled around the copper coin he always kept with him. Through the long years since he had been given the penny, he had acquired the habit of holding it in his hand whenever anything troubled him.

"Come here, Joshua," he said, stooping down to be on eye level with the boy. "I know how it feels to be without parents. I was as sorrowful as you until a kind lady gave me a new penny. It brought me good fortune, and that's why I call it my good luck penny."

He drew the coin slowly from his pocket and showed it to the boy. "Now it's yours," he said with a crooked grin. "Maybe it will bring you good fortune, too."

He pressed the penny into the boy's hand and curled the skinny, black fingers around it. "Keep it close to you as long as you need it, lad, and God bless you."

The boy didn't say a word—not even a thank you. But the sudden spark of life that came into those sorrowful brown eyes was all the thanks the captain needed.

He rose and watched the boy return to the cotton fields

46

with the field hand. Then he turned and walked slowly away from his good luck penny. He would miss it; his pocket already felt empty without it. But for some strange reason his heart was much lighter now than it had been when he started his walk up the riverbank.

Jeremy Roberts quickened his gait, and by the time he had reached the *Magnolia Belle,* he was whistling a happy tune.

BEN

1

A PREACHER'S comin'! A preacher's comin'!" The news traveled fast by the grapevine telegraph in the slave quarters of the Carver plantation.

It had been a long time since a preacher was allowed at the plantation. Ever since that black man, Nat Turner, had preached rebellion in Virginia, Mr. Carver had forbidden his Negroes to meet for Sunday school or church. But now that a white preacher was riding through the countryside, preaching to the black folks, Mr. Carver said it would be all right for his slaves to meet in the empty old slave cabin under the big oak tree.

On that bright Sunday morning in late March 1852, Joshua put on his best shirt of coarse tow and with his grandson, Ben, went to the empty slave cabin with the other slaves. With the overseer looking on, the white preacher

51

read carefully selected texts from the Bible.

"Blessed are the meek, for they shall inherit the earth."

"Servants, be obedient to them that are your masters."

When the overseer reported to Mr. Carver what the preacher's text was, the master was pleased and let the white preacher stay on for a while.

But when the moon was on the wane, the grapevine telegraph was busy with another message. As before, Joshua put on his best shirt of tow, but this time he did not take his grandson to the empty old slave cabin. He led Ben to the dark woods that lay beyond the cotton fields. When the oaks and hickorys closed around them, they joined the other slaves and all walked together through the forest until they came to an open space, lighted by a few smoking torches.

Ben looked around the clearing with wide eyes. There stood the tall preacher, John Parker, dressed in his black, long-tailed jacket and white starched shirt. By his side stood Big Joe and his young wife, Elizabeth.

Ben was glad that Big Joe wore his shirt tonight so that he couldn't see the field hand's bare back. Before he married Elizabeth, Big Joe had tried to escape to the North, but the overseer had brought him back in chains and had whipped him until he was almost dead. Ben and the other slave children shuddered every time they saw the long scars on Big Joe's broad back.

The meeting in the woods was different from the meeting in the slave quarters. This time when Mr. Parker opened his Bible, he read about the children of Israel in Egypt and their long fight for freedom. While he read, sharp-eared boys kept watch high up in the trees, ready to whistle like mocking birds if there was a sign of the overseer.

Ben had often heard the story of Moses before, but tonight Mr. Parker made the oppression of the children of

Israel seem like their own. He told how the Lord had finally persuaded King Pharaoh to let his slaves, the Israelites, go. "And then Moses led them out of Egypt to the Promised Land," the preacher said.

Murmurs of "Amen!" went around the gathering, and in her clear, sweet soprano voice Elizabeth broke into song:

> When Israel was in Egypt's land,
> Let my people go.
> Oppressed so hard they could not stand,
> Let my people go.

The others joined her in chorus, their voices a low, melodic murmur, blending with the wind through the trees.

> Go down, Moses,
> Way down in Egypt's land.
> Tell ole Pharaoh
> Let my people go.

After the preaching, John Parker told them about a place like the Promised Land called Canada. A queen ruled that land, and she made a law that all men should be free. There was no slavery in Canada, and anyone who could reach it would be a free person.

"How you get there?" one of the slaves asked.

"By following the North Star," John Parker replied. "Canada is a land far to the north."

When the meeting ended, the congregation broke up into small, separate groups and made their way back to the slave quarters in different directions. Ben followed his grandfather back the way they had come. When they came out of the woods, Ben asked, "How you know where to find that North Star Massa Parker told about?"

The old man stopped and pointed up to the sky. "See that

53

big Drinking Gourd up there, Ben?" The boy nodded when he had located the Big Dipper. "Well, the front end of that old Drinking Gourd points straight up to the North Star," Joshua told him.

Ben stopped and stared up at the bright star that pointed northward. "Granddaddy, the preacher said if you followed that star it would lead you to Canada, the Promised Land. If I followed the North Star would it take me there, too?"

And Joshua answered, "Yes, chile, it would."

> Go down, Moses,
> Way down in Egypt's land.
> Tell ole Pharaoh
> Let my people go.

Ben sang with the others as he hoed his row of cotton. Ever since Big Joe had tried to run away, the overseer insisted that the Negroes sing while they worked. Singing would keep the slaves from talking together, and when a slave sang, he'd be less likely to think about running away.

But the words of that old song stirred Ben's heart and made him think all the more about Canada. As he chopped the black soil with his hoe, he murmured the name over and over to himself. "Canada. Canada."

That day, while his grandson worked in the cotton fields, Joshua drove Massa Carver to town. When they returned, the coachman hurried to the slave quarters with disturbing news.

"Trader struttin' down the street in front of the courthouse, right past the slave auction block," Joshua said, his voice trembling. "An' I sees him talkin' with Massa. I couldn't hear what they was sayin' but I knows that every time Massa talks to a slave trader, it means trouble."

Big Joe frowned. "We best let the preacher know."

54

Late that night when the lights of the big house went out, Elizabeth slipped by Joshua's cabin singing: "When the old chariot come, I'm goin' to leave you . . . ."

The singing was a signal that there was a secret meeting in the woods.

Ben heard the singing from his straw mattress in a corner of the cabin. A short time later he heard Granddaddy Joshua blow out the candle and slip from the cabin into the dark night. He did not return until near morning.

The coming of Mr. Parker had put spirit into the hearts of the slaves, and the next day in the cotton fields Ben noticed that Big Joe sang as he never sang before.

> My Lord, he calls me,
> He calls me by the thunder,
> The trumpet sounds it in my soul,
> I ain't got long to stay here.

The overseer tapped out the rhythm of the old hymn on his hand with the handle of his bullwhip. He liked to hear the field hands sing so heartily. It meant that they were content with their lot.

When Ben returned to the slave quarters at the end of the day, his grandfather had a supper of corn meal mush and salt pork waiting for him. While the boy ate, Joshua talked about the meeting last night.

"Massa Parker's not only a preacher but he's an abolitionist," Joshua said. "That's a person who helps slaves get free, Ben. Massa Parker told us that he helps runaways get up north to Canada on the Underground Railroad."

"*Underground* Railroad?" Ben asked. He had never heard of a railroad built under the ground.

"Oh, it ain't a real railroad," Joshua replied with a chuckle. "Massa Parker says that's the name the abolitionists give to their secret way of helpin' slaves escape and get North. You see, it works like this, Ben. The guides that helps the runaways find their way to Canada is called 'conductors,' and the houses where the runaways is hidden is called 'stations.' The route the conductor takes is called the 'line,' and the fugitives is called 'passengers.' "

Joshua stopped talking, and the flickering flames in the small fireplace played over his dark, wrinkled face that had suddenly turned grave. After a long moment he spoke again in a low, sad voice. "You don't remember when you ma and daddy was sold. You was just a babe then, and the slave trader didn't want no babe, so you was left behind with me."

Ben had heard this story many times before, and he wondered why his grandfather should bring it up now.

"It's a fearsome thing to be sold downriver, boy," Joshua said, "and any time Massa Carver's gamblin' debts gets too much for him, us black folks has got to watch out. That's why your ma and daddy was sold downriver. Massa had a streak of bad luck gamblin' and had to get money fast, so he had to sell some of his slaves."

The old man paused and when he continued, his voice had the ring of fear in it. "Seein' massa talkin' to that slave trader in town got this ole head thinkin' that we is in for trouble again."

"What you mean?" Ben asked, alarmed. "Massa won't sell you, Granddaddy!"

"I knows, Ben," his grandfather answered him. "I'm too old and no slave trader wants an old slave. But you is a big strappin' boy and becomin' a good field hand. I seen Massa lookin' you over."

Ben drew in a quick breath. "You—you mean Massa'd sell me to the slave trader!"

"You ain't a little chile no longer, Ben. You is fourteen

56

years old and big for your age. Already you is doin' man's work." Joshua glanced down at his black gnarled hands. He seemed more sorrowful than ever, but when he looked up at his grandson again there was a spark of anger in his tired old eyes.

"I seen my own ma and daddy sold downriver when I was younger than you, Ben. Then I seen my son and his wife go off with the slave trader. But I ain't goin' to see my grandson sold downriver. No sir, boy, you is goin' *up* the river."

Frightened by his grandfather's words, Ben left the table and ran over to where the old man was sitting. "But, Granddaddy, I don't want to leave you."

Joshua curled his arm around his grandson. "And I don't want you to leave, either, chile. You's the only kinfolk I got, and I loves you. I'd keep you with me always if I could, but I knows I can't. I'd feel much better, and I knows you ma and daddy would, too, if you'd go up to Canada and be free."

"Canada!"

Joshua put a gnarled finger across his lips. "Don't say that word too loud, Ben. If Massa heard you say it, he'd have the overseer skin you alive."

"But—but—when?" Ben asked, dropping his voice to a whisper.

Joshua leaned over and murmured in the boy's ear, "Massa Parker knows the how and I knows the when." Then he told Ben about the meeting in the woods last night when Big Joe had asked Massa Parker if he could get him and Elizabeth to Canada.

"Massa Parker said he knowed a way," Joshua said, "and you can go with them, Ben."

Ben looked up at his grandfather with puzzled, frightened eyes. "But—but why is Big Joe runnin' away again after bein' whipped so bad the last time?" he asked. He shivered at the

57

thought of those long ugly scars across Big Joe's back. "Granddaddy, I don't want to be whipped like that."

"Big Joe went off by himself last time without nobody to guide him," Joshua explained. "This time he has Massa Parker and the Underground Railroad to help him. Big Joe knows that Massa Carver will be sure to sell him because Massa wants no runaways around. And Elizabeth's goin' with Big Joe because they be man and wife and don't ever want to be separated."

Joshua paused for a moment, then looked soberly at his grandson. "It's up to you, Ben. Runnin' away is full of dangers, even with the Underground Railroad to help you. I knows that. If you gets caught, you'll be whipped, but if you gets to Canada, you'll no longer be a slave. You'll be free for the rest of your life. Is you afraid to try it, boy?"

Ben nodded. "I'm afraid, Granddaddy, but I want to be free. I want to see that Promised Land Massa Parker talks about. I'll go with Big Joe and Elizabeth."

Joshua reached out and squeezed Ben's hand. "I knowed you would, boy. I seen the light in your eyes when Massa Parker talked about the Promised Land."

"When is we leavin'?" Ben asked.

"It be this Saturday night," Joshua said in a hushed voice. "Massa Carver's havin' a party at the big house, and there'll be so much noise and music up there that nobody's goin' hear footsteps sneakin' off."

"Saturday night—" Ben murmured. Then he drew in his breath. Saturday was only two days away.

He thought about little else than the plan for escape during the next two days. He wondered how long it would take Big Joe, Elizabeth, and him to get to Canada. What would the Promised Land be like? Would he really be free? He couldn't imagine how it would feel to be free. Maybe like that big old eagle back in the forest that soared high in the air and could settle in any tree it wanted to.

But Ben wished—oh, how he wished—that Granddaddy Joshua was going with him.

2

NIGHT SOUNDS droned through the slave quarters—the grumping of bullfrogs down by the river, the *clack, clack* of cicadas high in the trees, a restless wind through the branches of the big oak. From the big house came echoes of music, punctuated by strains of laughter. Joshua and Ben heard all these sounds as they sat quietly in their cabin, waiting.

At length the old man said, "We might as well talk to the Lord, Ben. It'll ease the waitin'."

He drew the boy to his knees beside him and in a low, respectful voice, he prayed, "Oh, Lord, please don't pass this black boy by. He be needin' your protection now. Lead him safe to the Promised Land like you done them Israelites in Egypt. Amen."

Talking to the Lord with Granddaddy always made Ben

feel good. But tonight he was too excited to feel much of anything. He just felt numb all over.

While they were still on their knees, Joshua reached deep into his pocket and drew out a copper coin. "A riverboat captain gave me this penny the day my ma and daddy was sold downriver," he told Ben. "The captain called it his good luck penny, and it brought me a good bit of comfort, too, these long, hard years."

Joshua put the penny into the palm of Ben's hand. Ben looked down at it. He turned it over and studied it thoughtfully. "There's writin' on it, Granddaddy," he said.

"I knows," Joshua replied. "One time I asked a black man who could read what it said, and he told me the writin' above the head was the word Liberty. I asked him what liberty meant, and he told me it meant freedom. I figured a coin with the word freedom on it was worth keepin' so I kept it all these years. Now it's yours, Ben. When the way gets hard, keep lookin' at that word Liberty, and it'll help you keep goin'."

Ben put the good luck penny into his ticking bag with his winter blanket, his shoes, and the extra hoecakes his grandfather had made for him for the journey. He tied the sack around his waist and slipped into his worn cotton jacket. Joshua blew out the candle, and they stood there in the dark.

"What for you blowed out the light?" asked Ben.

"So's I can't see you when you go, boy," the old man explained. "If I don't see you go, I won't have to lie when Massa Carver asks me if I seen you leave."

He stopped talking and stiffened. "Ben—listen! That be the signal."

They stood together, straining their ears. Close by a soft voice sang: "When that old chariot come, I'm goin' to leave you. . . ."

61

In a trembling voice Ben sang his reply: "When that old chariot come, I'm a-goin' with you."

Joshua reached out in the dark and clasped his grandson to him for the last time. Ben felt the old man's tears against his cheek, and his own eyes were moist. For a long moment Joshua held him tightly, then he gently pushed him through the cabin door and turned his back quickly so that he wouldn't see his grandson leave.

Elizabeth was waiting by the big oak. She wasn't singing now. When she saw Ben coming, she started out for the woods like a fleeting shadow.

Ben followed a short distance behind her. When he came to the end of the slave quarters, he turned to look back at his grandfather's cabin, the only home he had ever known. It was dark now, and the vision of his grandfather sitting alone and sorrowful rose up before him.

For a brief moment Ben felt like running back to the cabin and throwing himself into Granddaddy Joshua's arms as he had done so often when he was a small boy. The sobs rose in his throat and he shook all over. Then he swallowed hard and tried to pull himself together. He was almost a grown man now and he had a journey to make. He knew that if he were sold downriver like the rest of his family, Granddaddy Joshua would be more unhappy than he was now. So he turned quickly and followed Elizabeth's shadow across the fields.

When he reached the woods, she grasped his hand and together they hurried through the dark forest without speaking a word. When they reached the clearing, Mr. Parker and Big Joe were waiting for them. Guarded by the circle of big trees, the three gathered together in a tight little knot as they listened to what the preacher had to say.

"Tonight you will follow the Mississippi River north," Mr.

Parker told them. "With the river close by and the North Star to guide you, you can't get lost. Try to stay close together all the time. Travel only by night and rest well hidden by day.

He paused and looked earnestly at each one of them. "Your journey to freedom won't be an easy one, and if you're caught, you know the consequences. It's not too late to return to the slave quarters."

His gaze lingered on Ben as he spoke these words, but Ben didn't move a muscle. He looked back at the preacher without as much as blinking an eye.

Mr. Parker nodded. "Very well, then. Big Joe knows the route to Benton's Landing where I will meet you with a horse and wagon. I will be disguised so you may not recognize me, but you'll know me when I say, "Friends with a friend." That is the password on the Underground Railroad. Do not go along with anybody unless they speak those words. Be careful, but try to make as much time as you can tonight. Tomorrow is Sunday and the field hands won't be in the fields, so let's hope you won't be missed until Monday. That will give you a good day's lead."

He stopped talking and shook hands with each one of them. Ben had never shaken hands with a white man before and when Mr. Parker reached out for his hand, it was like a bridge leading to freedom.

"Now go quietly," the preacher warned. "I will go up to the big house so they will think nothing is amiss. Tomorrow I'll start out for Benton's Landing. God bless you."

He waited in the clearing while the three fugitives slipped through the dark forest. When he was sure they had reached the river without being seen, he hurried back to the plantation.

"Massa Parker is a good man," Big Joe spoke for the first

time when they paused for breath by the levee. "He make me see that not all white men are bad."

"Hush, we best not talk," Elizabeth warned. She straightened the blue headrag that was wound around her head, then followed her husband past the levee. Ben brought up the rear.

They hurried along the riverbank until the lights of the big house were out of sight, and the sounds of music and laughter faded into the night. Now only the fast-moving flow of the big Mississippi reached their ears, broken now and then by splashes of water over its eddies.

The river wound like a snake through the low delta. At one turn Big Joe didn't follow its course but plunged straight ahead through damp swamp grass. When Elizabeth questioned why they were going this way instead of following the bend in the river, Big Joe whispered back, "Massa Parker told me about the short cut through this old swamp, girl. He say when Massa Carver's slave catchers come chasin' after us, no bloodhound will smell our scent through water."

Ben hitched his ticking bag higher around his waist and followed Big Joe and Elizabeth through the swamp. Cold mud sucked at his bare feet, and coarse reeds whipped his legs and arms. The swamp was so dark that he could hardly see what was in front of him. Once he bumped into the water-knee protruding from a tall swamp cypress and had to grab the tree to steady himself. But he kept struggling on, splashing in the wake of Elizabeth.

When at last the ground under their feet became firm, Big Joe stopped, and Ben and Elizabeth leaned against the trees to rest. Ben looked up at the stars and found the Drinking Gourd with the bright North Star ahead of it. He wondered how many nights they would be following that bright star.

All too soon Big Joe motioned them on, and they started out again toward the riverbank.

"I smells catfish in that river," Big Joe said. "Maybe tomorrow mornin' while the mist is hangin' over the water I can catch us some."

Elizabeth, who knew how much Big Joe liked to fish, reminded him, "We got our rations with us. Best to think about fishin' when we reach the freedom land."

As they hurried along, Elizabeth hummed old hymns, and Ben found that the rhythm of her singing made his steps lighter.

Didn't my Lord deliver Daniel?
Deliver Daniel, deliver Daniel,
Didn't my Lord deliver Daniel,
And why not every man?

When a faint glow showed on the eastern horizon and the North Star faded, Big Joe led them away from the riverbank to a little stream in a patch of woods. Near the stream wild grapevines looped around the trees and bushes, making dark leafy tunnels through the brush. The vines were so thick that Big Joe had to break an opening through them.

"This be a good place to hide away durin' the day," he said. He took Elizabeth's gourd and handed it to Ben. "Get us some water, Ben."

When Ben returned from the stream, Big Joe motioned for him to squeeze between the opening in the vines. After Ben pushed his way through the vines, Big Joe pulled the opening together again and they found themselves in a snug, leafy shelter.

"I'll stay on guard until sunhigh," Big Joe said. "Then, Ben, you and Elizabeth can take turns watching until night-fall. Now let's have some of that food."

65

Before she opened her sack, Elizabeth bowed her head. "Thank you, Lord, that we made it safe this far," she prayed. "And keep watch over us when Massa Carver finds us gone an' sends the slave catchers lookin' for us."

Ben shivered at the word slave catchers. He tried to hide his fear by taking a long drink from the drinking gourd. The water was cold and sweet, and after drinking his fill, Elizabeth opened her sack and gave them each a portion of bread and cold meat. The remainder she tied up inside the sack again.

When Ben finished eating, he lay down on the soft mossy ground. His feet were sore and bruised and his whole body ached. He was numbed with weariness; yet he couldn't go to sleep right away. He kept thinking about Granddaddy Joshua this early morning, sitting alone in the little cabin.

Remembering what his grandfather had said about the good luck penny, Ben reached into his ticking bag and brought out the coin. Now, he decided, was one of the times the going was hard—his first day away from Granddaddy Joshua and missing him so much.

In the faint morning light that shone through the vines, Ben looked long and hard at the word Liberty engraved on the coin. Then holding the penny tightly in his hand for comfort, he forgot all else and fell sound asleep.

3

IT SEEMED that he had been asleep only a short time when Elizabeth awakened him. "It's your turn to watch now, Ben. Keep your eyes and ears open, and if you sees or hears anything strange, you wake us."

Ben yawned and nodded.

"Now don't you go to sleep again," Elizabeth warned.

"I won't. I promise," Ben answered.

Elizabeth lay down next to Big Joe, who was snoring softly on his bed of moss. Ben crept to the opening in the vines and peered out. By the length of the shadows in the woods, he figured it was the middle of the afternoon. He'd have several hours to watch before sundown.

He leaned back against the opening in the vines and yawned again. Then he shook himself. It wouldn't do to doze off; he had to stay alert and keep watch. But outside the leafy hut the forest was so peaceful that it was hard to keep awake, and for the first time in his life Ben wished he had something to do.

He glanced down at his calloused hands and discovered that he still had the good luck penny clutched tightly in one of them. He opened his fingers and examined the coin closely.

He wondered who the lady was on the penny and why she was holding the funny-looking cap on a stick over her shoulder. His eyes fell on the word Liberty above the head, and he traced the letters with his finger. Someday he'd like to learn to read so that he'd know what each letter meant. Maybe in Canada they taught black boys to read. He hoped so.

Ben put the penny into his sack and peered through the opening in the vines again. A breeze wafted the sweet smell of honeysuckle past his leafy shelter. The stream gurgled softly as it wound its way through the trees. He saw a spotted fawn and its mother drop their graceful heads to the water to drink. A mockingbird sang loudly in a bush nearby.

Suddenly the bird fluttered off through the trees, leaving the woods empty of its song. The doe and fawn raised their heads, their pointed ears wide and alert. Obeying an ancient instinct, they leaped across the stream and vanished like shadows into the woods.

Ben sat tense and listened. Only after a long moment did he hear what the deer had heard. Far away it was but coming closer, the baying of dogs in the distance.

He scrambled back from the opening in the vines and reached out in the semidarkness of the hut to shake Elizabeth's shoulder. "Listen!" he cried.

Elizabeth's eyes shot open, and her body popped up in a sitting position as if a spring had been attached to it.

"Bloodhounds!" she gasped. She shook Big Joe awake, and hurriedly they gathered their sacks together. A short time later they were out of their leafy refuge and heading toward the stream.

"Walk in the middle," Big Joe ordered. "The water will kill our scent." He dragged Elizabeth along in his hurry to put distance behind them and the baying dogs. Ben splashed after them.

As they made their way upstream through the cold water, they kept straining their ears for the sounds of the dogs. At one point the barking became a series of high-pitched howls. Big Joe paused a moment to listen.

"They found our hiding place," he said. "That's what's makin' 'em all excited. Come on!"

They struggled through the cold stream until the howling became fainter and fainter. When they heard it no more, they stopped along the bank to catch their breath.

"They ain't following us no longer. Thank the Lord for that," Big Joe said. "Now we got to find our way back to the river." He examined the trunks of the trees around them, and Ben wondered what he was doing.

"Massa Parker told me how to find directions in the day when there's no North Star to guide us," Big Joe explained. "He said to look at what side of a tree trunk the moss grows thickest. That's north. I reckon this old stream twisted us inland away from the river, so we got to head north and east." He pointed the way through the trees, and they started out in that direction.

As they hurried along, Ben still kept alert for the baying of the hounds, but all was quiet. Finally they reached the river where they hid along the bank until nightfall.

"Do you reckon them bloodhounds belong to Massa Carver's slave catchers?" Elizabeth whispered fearfully.

"They be his or belong to another slave catcher huntin'
for runaways," Big Joe replied.

Ben felt a cold chill crawl down his spine as the thought of
that horrible baying sound. Being a fugitive wasn't as excit-
ing as he had thought it would be. It was downright
frightening!

They ate some cold hoecakes and washed them down
with fishy-tasting river water. When the sun sank behind a
dark cloud bank in the west, they crept from the bushes and
started out again. But as night deepened, clouds stretched
across the sky, blotting out the Big Dipper and the North
Star.

"We has nothing but the river to guide us now," Big Joe
warned, "so stick close." His big body was blurred by darkness. Ben could scarcely see him.

Elizabeth suggested that they take hands so that they
wouldn't get separated, and hand in hand they crept along
the riverbank. When they came to settlements along the
river, they huddled close to the bank and moved cautiously.
Once a farm dog chased them, and Ben's heart was in his
throat until Elizabeth tossed it a hoecake and it quieted
down.

"How do we know when we gets to Benton's Landing?"
Ben asked when they stopped to rest for a few minutes.

"Massa Parker says there's a signboard along the river
landing with the name on it," Big Joe answered.

Sometime during the night it began to rain, but they
didn't stop to take shelter. Big Joe kept dragging them along
until Ben thought he would drop. It was in the first light of
dawn when Elizabeth give his hand a squeeze and pointed
ahead.

"Yonder's a river landin' and a signboard. Let's see what
it say."

"How can we?" asked Ben as they crept close to the signboard. "None of us can read."

Big Joe pulled a piece of paper from his pocket and frowned down at it. "Massa Parker printed the name Benton's Landin' for me so's I can compare it with the name on the sign."

"It looks just like it to me," Elizabeth whispered, glancing down at the slip of paper in Big Joe's hand, then up at the name on the board. "All the letters go the same way an' they is all in the right order."

"An' both words has the same number of letters in them," added Ben, pleased that he could count so well.

"Then this here's the place," Big Joe said, stuffing the slip of paper back into his pocket and looking around him. "Massa Parker said we was to hide in a canebrake right across from the landin' until he comes for us. He told me he'd be drivin' a wagon, and he'd call three times like an old whippoorwill, so listen sharp for that call."

He led the way back from the riverbank, and they crossed the road that led to a cluster of houses north of the landing. Just as Mr. Parker had said there was a canebrake directly across from the landing. They made their way deep into the cane, but not too deep so that they couldn't see the road. The rain had stopped and the sky brightened while they sat shivering in their damp clothes, waiting for Mr. Parker's wagon.

"I be thankful when we is on that Underground Railroad," Elizabeth whispered uneasily. "It's a fearsome thing to be runnin' from the slave catchers alone." Ben and Big Joe nodded their weary heads in agreement.

As the day brightened, two men on horseback clattered up the road in the direction of the village. Next came a farm wagon. The three fugitives in the canebrake examined the wagon closely. But the driver gave no sign of knowing they were there, and the wagon went on up the road.

"You think Massa Parker's been here, and not findin' us, he left?" Elizabeth worried. "Runnin' from them hound dogs slowed us up some."

Big Joe shook his head. "He would have waited for us. Now we just got to be patient an' wait for him."

Ben was so exhausted from the long night's trek that he had to fight hard to keep from nodding. Even so, he was the first one to hear a whippoorwill call three times from down the road.

He was about to jump out of the canebrake and run to meet Mr. Parker when Big Joe pulled him back by the seat of the pants. "Keep down and hush!" Big Joe said sharply.

They heard the wagon before they saw it. It sounded just like the tin peddler's wagon that stopped twice a year at Massa Carver's big house. When the driver pulled the horse to a stop by the landing, the three fugitives stared with surprise. The man didn't look at all like Mr. Parker. He wore a broadbrimmed hat with untidy white hair hanging out from under it. He was shabbily dressed and had a dirty-looking, long gray beard.

The three waited tensely while the driver got down from his wagon to rearrange some of his wares.

"He's not Massa Parker," Elizabeth whispered, a look of concern flitting across her tired face. "He's just an old peddler."

"Massa Parker said we may not know him when he comes," Big Joe reminded her. "Let's just watch and see what he does."

Breathlessly they watched the peddler as he left his wagon and walked to the edge of the canebrake. He paused for a moment, looking furtively up and down the road. Then in a low voice that had a familiar ring to it, he said, "Friends with a friend."

With relief Big Joe answered with the same words. The peddler walked in the direction of Big Joe's voice. When he found them hidden in the cane, he ducked down beside them. Ben stared with surprise at the man. Nobody would have guessed it was the young preacher. Only the twinkling blue eyes and the voice were the same.

"I'm glad you made it here safely," Mr. Parker told them. "We can't talk now. I'll drive my peddler's wagon to that empty barn on the other side of the canebrake and meet you there. I'll be inside the barn. Knock three times on the door. That's the signal for the Underground Railroad."

"How do we reach the barn without bein' seen?" Big Joe asked.

"Cut across the cane," Mr. Parker said. "If you walk westward, away from the landing, you'll be in the right direction." And saying nothing more, he slipped out of the canebrake and was off down the road in his peddler's wagon.

Following his advice, they made their way across the canebrake and were soon on the other side. While Ben and Elizabeth remained hidden, Big Joe slipped out of the cane and went to the barn. He knocked three times on the door. It opened at once, and Mr. Parker waved them in.

After shutting and bolting the door behind them, Mr. Parker took off his hat, his long-haired wig, and his false beard. Ben drew a sigh of relief. "I'm glad it's really you, Massa Parker," he said.

The preacher laughed. "Now you know my two disguises. Sometimes I'm a preacher and sometimes a peddler. I had to leave the Carver Plantation as a peddler because your disappearance was discovered too quickly."

The three exchanged puzzled glances. "How'd Massa

find out so soon we was missin'?" Big Joe asked.

"Elizabeth was called to the big house to help clean up after the party," Mr. Parker said as he walked to the back of his wagon, "and when she wasn't found they hunted for you, Big Joe. When they couldn't find you either, they took a count of the slaves and discovered that Ben was missing too. Of course nobody in the slave quarters knew what happened to you, so Mr. Carver figured you three ran away and that I helped you."

There was a moment's silence as the fugitives looked fearfully at one another. So the bloodhounds they had heard yesterday had belonged to Massa Carver's slave catchers, Ben thought with a shudder. Like Elizabeth he was glad that Massa Parker was with them now and that they would soon be on the Underground Railroad.

"Mr. Carver's slave catchers won't give up easily," Mr. Parker continued. "They'll be looking for a field hand, his wife, a grown boy, and a preacher who's guiding them north. That's why I had to disguise myself as an old tin peddler. I can disguise Elizabeth and Ben, too, but you, Big Joe, will have to be hidden in the wagon."

Mr. Parker rummaged through the contents of the wagon as if he were hunting for something. At last he drew out a long box which he opened. He shuffled through several women's dresses, then selected two high-necked black ones with long sleeves. "Slip these on over your clothes," he told Elizabeth and Ben.

Ben stared with amazement at the woman's dress Mr. Parker held up to him. "You want that *I* should wear that?" he exclaimed. "I can't wear no woman's dress."

"Yes you can," Mr. Parker said. "Now take off your jacket and try it on."

Big Joe put a hand over his mouth to smother a giggle as

74

Mr. Parker pulled the dress over Ben's shoulders. He put a bonnet on the boy's head, with a heavy veil that hid his face, and handed him a pair of black cotton gloves.

"Why glory be, Ben," Elizabeth said with surprise. "You don't look like a black boy at all now."

"And that's just what we want," Mr. Parker told Ben. "Isn't it better to wear a woman's dress than to get caught by the slave catchers?"

"I reckon so," Ben mumbled from behind the heavy veil.

While Elizabeth got into her black dress and bonnet, Mr. Parker led Big Joe to the back of the wagon. "I have a hiding place just big enough for one person," he said, sliding his fingers between two of the planks on the floor of the wagon. He pulled them open on hidden hinges.

"Now ain't that somethin'!" Big Joe exclaimed as he stared down at the hidden compartment with amazement.

"I'm afraid it will be a bit cramped and not the most comfortable way to travel," Mr. Parker told him, "but I've carried other men as big as you in there, and they all survived."

"If we gets to the Promised Land, I don't care how I travel," Big Joe said as he hoisted himself up onto the wagon and wriggled into the hollow space beneath the false bottom. When Big Joe was settled, Mr. Parker pushed the planks down together and put the box of dresses over them. Then he quickly put on his wig, false beard, and hat and helped Elizabeth and Ben onto the wagon seat. He unbolted the barn door and peered out.

"The coast is clear," he said as he led the big gray horse out of the barn. He climbed up next to Elizabeth and Ben and clucked to the horse. With a rattle of pots and pans they jolted down the lane toward the river landing.

4

BEN SQUIRMED uncomfortably in the long black dress as they waited at Benton's Landing for the steam ferry to take them across the river. The heavy veil that hid his face seemed stifling, and he kept blowing it away from his nose. Elizabeth had to nudge him to sit quietly.

At last the ferry came, and for the first time in his life Ben crossed the big yellow Mississippi to its eastern shore. Through his veil he could make out the distant shore, drawing nearer and nearer. He wondered what lay beyond the low blue hills on the far horizon. Well, he would soon find out, and for the first time since running away from the Carver plantation, Ben felt a thrill of adventure.

As soon as the ferry reached the landing, Mr. Parker paid the ferryman and they headed away from the river for the open country. As they rattled up the red clay road, Mr.

Parker told Ben and Elizabeth why they had left the river to go overland.

"Mr. Carver's slave catchers will be hunting for you on both sides of the Mississippi," he said. "Runaways usually follow the river to get North."

"Where we bound for now?" asked Elizabeth.

"I'm taking you as far as Memphis, Tennessee," Mr. Parker replied. "At Memphis I'll see that you get on a steamboat for Louisville, Kentucky. Now if anybody stops us," he warned, "don't say a word. Let me do all the talking."

They rode along in silence for a while, past farms and skirting small villages. At one point on their journey, where the road curved and a large white farmhouse came into view, Mr. Parker let the reins fall slack and turned his head toward the farm.

"I used to live in a house like that," he told them, his voice sounding wistful. "Up in Virginia."

Elizabeth leaned over to look at the peddler. "You come from the South, Massa?" she asked with surprise.

Mr. Parker nodded. "I guess it sounds strange for a Southerner to be helping runaway slaves, but not all Southerners like slavery. Some of the strongest abolitionists come from the South."

He took up the reins again and urged the horse to a faster trot. "The 'president' of the Underground Railroad came from North Carolina," he went on. "His name is Levi Coffin and he's a Quaker storekeeper in Cincinnati. He hated slavery as a boy, and he's so opposed to it now that he won't sell any goods in his store that have been made by slave labor. They call him 'president' of the Underground Railroad because the slave catchers have never yet caught a runaway who has come to him. They say that about a

77

hundred fugitives pass through his house a year."

"A hundred fugitives!" exclaimed Ben. "That's a lot of slaves to hide in a year."

Mr. Parker nodded solemnly. "Yes it is, Ben, but it's worth the effort to help so many folks to freedom."

As the peddler's wagon rattled on, Ben wondered how Big Joe was faring in the hidden compartment under the false wagon bottom, and when Mr. Parker stopped along a lonely country lane to let poor Joe stretch his legs, Ben decided that wearing a woman's dress and bonnet wasn't as bad as being cramped in that stuffy hole.

Now and then a farmer's wife hailed them from the side of the road, and Mr. Parker stopped to show her his wares. Then Ben was thankful for the heavy black veil that hid his face, especially when the farmer's wife turned her head in his direction. When she did this, Ben sat as quietly as he could beside Elizabeth so as not to attract attention to himself.

At one stop when a curious woman asked about the "two ladies" riding with the peddler, Mr. Parker told her that he was taking his sister and niece to a funeral in a nearby town. The woman paid Mr. Parker for the broom she bought and gave the two passengers a sad, respectful nod. Quickly Mr. Parker flicked the reins over the back of the big gray horse and they were on their way again.

"I don't like to tell falsehoods," he said when they were out of earshot of the farmer's wife, "but sometimes it is necessary on the Underground Railroad. And to me an innocent falsehood isn't as bad as risking a human life."

It was getting dark when they stopped again, this time at a red brick farmhouse which Mr. Parker said was a "station" on the Underground Railroad. Ben, Big Joe, and Elizabeth were hurried into a large cheerful kitchen where a table was set for supper. The farmer's wife nodded that they should sit down at the table. Soon plates heaped with chicken, mashed potatoes, and greens were set before them. Ben had never eaten so much good food before, and after a second helping of cherry pie, he beamed a smile of satisfaction at the farmer's wife.

When the meal was over, they were secreted to the barn where they slept in the loft. Before daybreak the next morning they were on their way again.

Because they had to stop so often to sell the peddler's wares, it took them four days to reach Memphis. Mr. Parker drove the wagon down a side street to the river, where the long stone levee was bustling with activity. Rivermen were loading and unloading the big freight boats, and noise and confusion filled the air. Men shouted orders, ship bells clanged, and the whistle of a passenger steamer blew shrilly as the boat edged toward the levee.

Amid the confusion of passengers leaving the boat, Mr. Parker hurried his own passengers from the peddler's wagon to a Mississippi River steamer, where an abolitionist captain would take them up the river to Louisville. As soon as he saw that they were safely on board, Mr. Parker said good-bye to his passengers and wished them Godspeed. Ben felt a lump in his throat as he shook Mr. Parker's hand for the last time. He would miss their friend who had done so much for them.

Captain Weber led the fugitives into the hold of his boat where the cargo was stored and told them to stay hidden behind the stacked bales of cotton. Ben was happy to shed his long dress, dark veil, and hat, and Big Joe was relieved to be able to stretch his cramped arms and legs again. When the captain brought them their supper that night, he told them that they would be starting up the river the next day.

In the morning the shrill blast from the boat whistle

awakened Ben, and he listened excitedly as the paddle wheels began to turn, pushing them upriver toward Louisville.

The long days that followed seemed to string together endlessly for the fugitives hidden in the hold. On dark nights Ben and Big Joe were able to go on deck to help the black roustabouts, but poor Elizabeth had nothing to do but stay hidden and wait. She bided her time with patience. Massa Parker had told them that their journey to freedom wouldn't be an easy one, and Elizabeth was determined not to complain.

One night when Captain Weber brought them their supper, he said, "Tomorrow we'll reach Cairo, Kentucky, where the Ohio River joins the Mississippi. From Cairo we'll travel up the Ohio to Louisville. It won't be long now."

At Cairo they stopped to unload some cargo and take on a few passengers. Then up the Ohio they went, and several days later they arrived in Louisville.

A wagon drew up along the levee and several bales of cotton and three passengers were loaded on it and covered with a heavy tarpaulin. The wagon made its way through the side streets of Louisville to an old warehouse. In back of the warehouse was another wagon which took the human freight to a farmhouse outside the city, where a warm meal awaited them.

That night they slept in the hayloft of the barn. It was good to be out of that dark, damp hold of the riverboat and into a warm, dry barn again. Ben stretched his arms in contentment and snuggled down deep into the sweet-smelling hay.

In seconds he was fast asleep, but several hours later he was awakened by someone shaking him. Opening his eyes, he stared into the dark, not sure where he was for a moment.

Then Big Joe shook his shoulder again and whispered harshly, "Get up, Ben. We got to leave at once."

Ben sat up and blinked at the farmer who was perched on the ladder at the edge of the hayloft. In the glow of the lantern he was holding, his face had a tense, worried look. "Word came tonight that Mr. Parker has been arrested," he told them. "It seems that he was seen leaving the Carver plantation as a peddler, and Mr. Carver's slave catchers caught up with him in Memphis."

Elizabeth sucked in her breath; in the light of the lantern her dark eyes flashed with horror. "What they fixin' to do to poor Massa Parker," she whispered.

"He'll be fined and put in jail," the farmer replied. "But it's not the first time he's been jailed for helping runaways escape, and it most likely won't be the last. Now get your things; we best be puttin' as many miles behind us as we can before sunup."

"Where we goin'?" Big Joe asked, his deep voice quivering.

"I'm taking you to Sims' Landing where you'll meet a lumber raft crossing the river to Ohio. From there the Underground Railroad will take you to Cincinnati. It's all been arranged, but we got to hurry before those slave catchers trace you to this barn."

"Isn't Cincinnati where Massa Levi Coffin lives?" Ben asked as he followed the farmer down the ladder.

The man nodded.

Ben's face broke into a wide grin. "When we reach Ohio, we'll be in the North."

"That's right," the farmer replied, "but you aren't any safer in the state of Ohio than you are here in Kentucky. With the new Fugitive Slave Law, slave catchers can catch you as easily in the North now as in the South. And all

Northerners are required by law to turn in runaway slaves. They'll be put in jail and fined $1,000 if they don't."

"So, as Massa Parker said, we got to get all the way to Canada to be safe," Big Joe added.

While the men hitched the team of horses to the wagon, Elizabeth went to the farmhouse for the basket of food the farmer's wife was preparing for them. As soon as she returned to the wagon, they started out, and by the time the sun came up they were miles away from Louisville and the farm.

It was the middle of the day when they reached Sims' Landing. Ben peeked out from under the heavy canvas that hid them. He glimpsed several small fishing boats and a ferryboat tied to the landing. Back from it were a few houses and barns, but nobody seemed to be about the small settlement.

The farmer drove his team past the landing and around a bend in the road. When he pulled the horses to a stop by a dark copse of trees, he called softly from the wagon seat, "Beyond those trees along the riverbank is a cave. You're to hide there until sundown. Then keep your eyes open for a lumber raft that will come into the cove to pick you up. The man who is poling the raft will be wearing a bright blue cap. He'll take you across the river to Ohio. Now get out and hide in—"

He was interrupted suddenly by a loud clop-clop of hoofbeats coming from around the bend.

"Hurry! Get out and hide in those trees," the farmer cried. "I'll try to head them off."

The three fugitives threw back the canvas and scrambled off the wagon. With Ben in the lead they ran for the riverbank. They had just reached the cover of trees when three riders came into view around the bend.

They stopped their horses by the farm wagon, and one of the men with a silver badge pinned to his coat spoke to the farmer. "I'm Sheriff Henderson. What you hauling and where you headin' for?"

"You can see my wagon's empty," the farmer replied. "I'm heading upriver for a load of seed corn."

The sheriff flipped his head toward the two riders by his side. They were burly-looking fellows with pistols in their belts. One had a bullwhip coiled over his saddle horn. Ben shivered when he saw that.

"My friends here have come all the way from down the Mississippi, huntin' three runaways from the Carver Plantation," Sheriff Henderson explained. "They're worth five hundred dollars each, and we aim to catch 'em and return 'em to their rightful owner."

The farmer shook his head as if he didn't know anything about the matter.

"Well, if you see 'em leave word along the river," the sheriff said, "and we'll pick 'em up."

The farmer nodded and flapped his reins over the horses' backs. The wagon went on down the road with the two slave catchers following.

Sheriff Henderson remained behind and stared intently at the copse of trees. It seemed to the three frightened fugitives that he was staring right at them. They stood tense and shaken, hardly daring to breathe.

Finally the sheriff turned his horse around and rode back to Sims' Landing. The three stood frozen until the man and horse were out of sight; then in a strained voice Big Joe said, "That was a close one. We best head for that cave an' stay hidden."

Stealthily they crept down the riverbank. At the edge of the river, in a quiet little cove, they found a shallow cave.

They pressed back into its dark shadows to wait for sun-down.

Ben had never thought that time could pass so slowly. With the slave catchers and the sheriff close by, he wished that sundown would hurry along. He leaned back against a stone ledge in the cave and kept his ears open for the sharp clop-clop of horses' hoofs that might signal the return of the slave catchers. An unnatural silence hung over the cave, as if the woods and the river were waiting, too, and listening. Even the pounding of his heart seemed loud to Ben in the hush around them.

With a long sigh he reached down and untied the ticking bag around his waist. With trembling hands he fished inside it for the good luck penny. As he drew the coin from the bag, his grandfather's words came back to him.

"When the way gets hard, keep lookin' at that word Liberty, and it'll help you keep goin'."

Ben looked at his good luck penny long and hard, then closed his hand tightly around it.

Every now and then Big Joe ventured out of the cave to listen and to watch. But the woods behind them remained ominously quiet.

When finally the shadows stretched along the riverbank and the sunset stained the water in long red streaks, Big Joe said, "Now we got to watch for that lumber raft."

Ben slipped the penny back into his ticking bag and crawled to the entrance of the cave with Big Joe and Elizabeth. They kept their eyes on the river, carefully studying every boat that passed. Suddenly Big Joe, who had been watching the shadowy shoreline, drew in a quick breath and grabbed Elizabeth's arm. "There it be!"

Ben crouched forward to get a better look at the big raft that was slowly coming downstream. It had a stack of lumber on it and was being poled by a young man wearing a bright blue cap over his long blond hair. The raft was about to nose into the little cove when the silence of the woods was shattered by the barking of dogs.

"Oh, Lawdy," Big Joe gasped, "the slave catchers has come back and brought the dogs with them!"

At the sound of the hounds the raftsman quickly poled his raft back into the current.

At that split second Big Joe leaped out of the cave. "Wait! Wait!" he cried. Then at the top of his voice he shouted, "Friends with a friend."

At the sound of those words, the young man stopped the raft and stared into the shadows of the cove. At the same moment one of the dogs broke out of the woods above the cave.

"Quick, jump into the water!" the raftsman shouted. "I'll hold the raft steady. Swim out to it."

Big Joe seized Elizabeth by the arm and dragged her into the water after him. They waded across the cove until the water became deep and Big Joe had to swim with Elizabeth to the raft.

"Come on! Come on!" the raftsman urged Ben.

Ben swallowed hard and looked down at the dark water. He didn't know how to swim. He stood frozen like a statue, staring at the river with terror-filled eyes.

It was the gunshot that echoed through the woods behind him that forced Ben to leap into the cold water. He splashed across the cove until his feet couldn't touch bottom and he found himself struggling in deep water. He was halfway to the raft when he went under, the raftman's words still ringing in his ears. "Hurry! Swim—"

Amid a flurry of air bubbles, Ben fought his way to the surface of the water, gasping for breath. He thrashed about in the murky river but was dragged under again by the current. His head bobbed up, his arms smacking the surface of the water. He would have gone under a third time if a hand hadn't grabbed him just in time. Coughing and sputtering for breath, he felt Big Joe's strong arm around him, towing him the rest of the way across the cove.

Big Joe pushed Ben's limp body onto the raft, then managed to swing onto it himself just as a bullet spattered the water close by.

"Hide behind that pile of lumber," the raftsman shouted; then pushing hard on his pole, he turned the raft into the swift current. And none too soon. From behind the pile of lumber where he lay frightened and exhausted, Ben could hear the angry shouts of the slave hunters. In his mind's eye he could see them shaking their fists at the departing raft. Shivering in his wet clothes, he listened to their curses and harsh threats fade into the night.

The raft sped downriver with the current. When the young man thought it was safe to turn it, he steered across the river toward the opposite shore. Big Joe found another pole and added his strength to guiding the raft across the currents. Soon the dark outline of the Ohio shore appeared before them, coming closer and closer, and Ben let out a deep, shuddering sigh of relief.

They followed the shore northward for several miles until they came to a crude landing. Here the young raftsman tied up his craft and hurried the fugitives up the riverbank to a waiting horse-drawn cart. A man in city clothes sat nodding on the driver's seat. When he heard them coming, he straightened up quickly, got down from his high perch, and pulled out the large drawers that were built all around the wagon.

"I'm a roaming bookbinder," he said, speaking low and

86

quickly. "Get in the center behind the drawers and stay quiet."

As the drawers closed in on them, the last thing Ben glimpsed was the blue cap of the raftsman melting into the dark night. In an instant they were jostling back and forth in their cramped hiding place. Ben was still shivering in his wet clothes, but a thick blanket underneath him warmed him, and slowly his tight muscles began to relax.

"If all goes well," came the words from the wagon seat above, "we'll reach Cincinnati by morning."

5

How long he had been asleep Ben had no idea. But when the bookbinder's wagon came to a sudden stop and the swaying ceased, Ben's eyes shot wide open. The removal of the drawers made him blink up into the pale blue of early morning.

At the driver's command the three fugitives crawled stiffly out of the wagon and followed him to the back door of a large frame house. The driver knocked three times and called softly, "Friends with a friend."

The door opened at once, and a tall man stepped aside so that they could enter. He motioned them all into the house with a rapid sweep of his hand.

"Friend Coffin, I have brought thee three passengers bound for Canada," the bookbinder said. Ben stared up at the man who quickly closed the door behind them. So this was Levi Coffin, "president" of the Underground Railroad.

Mr. Coffin wore the short knee britches of a Quaker and a long gray coat with no collar. He was a tall, thin man with gray hair and a long, narrow face which gave him a stern appearance. But when Ben gazed into the bright blue eyes, he saw compassion and kindness.

In turn the tall Quaker studied the three ragged fugitives who stood like bent reeds before him. Big Joe's wide shoulder had burst through a seam in his shirt, and there was a long tear in the knee of his trousers. Elizabeth had lost her blue headrag in her swim in the river, and her coarse cotton shift was smeared with river mud. Ben's own shirt and pants were muddy rags.

It was while he was examining himself with downcast eyes that Ben realized that his ticking bag was no longer tied around his waist. In the excitement of escaping from the slave catchers, he had left it and his good luck penny in the cave on the Kentucky side of the Ohio River.

A wave of dismay came over him, but there was no time to think about the lost penny now. Mr. Coffin was leading them across the kitchen toward a plump, smiling woman who had just entered the room. "Catherine, we have three new passengers traveling our railroad," he told her.

Mrs. Coffin nodded a greeting at the runaways and motioned for them to follow her into the washroom next to the kitchen. After they had scrubbed off the river mud, she led them to another room where there was a large closet full of clean clothes.

Ben felt like a different person in his new white shirt and pants. There were even three pairs of shoes to go around, and Mrs. Coffin handed each one of them a warm sweater. "Thee will need sweaters in Canada this time of year," she said.

Back in the kitchen breakfast awaited them, and after they had eaten Mr. Coffin whisked them off to a hidden cellar under his store, which adjoined the house. They followed him through a dark passageway until they came to a heavy wooden door. Mr. Coffin opened the door and beckoned them inside.

Ben looked around with amazement. They were in a large cellar room with gray stone walls and an earthen floor. The room was furnished with cots and a long trestle table with high-backed chairs. There were no windows, but a warm fire in a small hearth provided a cheerful light.

"Thee will have to remain here until the way is clear to get thee to Cleveland," Mr. Coffin told them. "The Friend who brought thee to my house told me about the close escape thee had across the river. The slave catchers will be suspicious and will be watching my house and store, so thee cannot leave until we are sure they have gone."

"When we gets to Cleveland will we be in Canada?" Big Joe asked.

"No, Cleveland is still in Ohio," Mr. Coffin replied. "But at Cleveland a boat will take thee across Lake Erie to Canada."

He looked around the room to see if everything was in order, then said, "I must go up to my store now. Catherine will look in on thee to see if thee need anything. Be sure to bolt the door after I leave and do not open it unless there are three knocks and the password is given."

He looked at them gravely for a moment; then his long, solemn face broke into a gentle smile. "Thee will be safe here," he assured them.

After he closed the door behind him and Big Joe secured it with the iron bolt, Ben flung himself on one of the cots and sighed wearily. It was good not to be running from slave catchers for the moment, and he decided he would just lie here all day and sleep.

When he finally awoke, he sensed it was late in the day. Big Joe and Elizabeth were sitting at the trestle table, talking in low tones. Ben went over to join them.

"While you was sleepin', Ben, Massa Coffin came to warn us to be quiet," Big Joe told him. "The sheriff was here with the slave catchers to search this house."

At Big Joe's words Ben felt a hot throb of fear, and his courage seemed to ebb right out through his feet. He looked down at his empty hands and longed for the feel of his good luck penny in them. But with quick anguish he remembered that it was at the bottom of his ticking bag in the cave at Sims' Landing.

Seeing his baleful look, Elizabeth asked, "What's the matter, Ben? Is you upset about what Joe just told you?"

Ben nodded bleakly. "And something else, too," he said and told them about his lost penny.

Elizabeth reached over and touched his hand gently. "We is safe here, Ben," she said, "so don't you fret no more about that old penny."

"It's not just an old penny," Ben told her. "It's a good luck penny that belonged to my granddaddy. He gave it to me the night we run away, and now it's on the other side of the river."

"Well, I know your granddaddy would rather have you safe on this side of the river without the penny," Elizabeth said. "Besides, you won't be needin' a good luck penny much longer, Ben. Massa Parker told us that Massa Coffin has never lost a runaway yet. We is in his hands, now, and with the good Lord's help, he'll get us into the Promised Land."

"If he don't get arrested like Massa Parker," Big Joe muttered grimly. In the next breath he added, "Why you reckon some white folks like Massa Parker and Massa Coffin risk gettin' themselves put in jail for us runaways?"

Elizabeth raised her head and looked at her husband. "Because, as Massa Parker told us, the Bible says all men are brothers, and it ain't right to let your brothers get bought and sold into slavery. The Lord don't like it, and good folks like Massa Parker and Massa Coffin don't like it either."

Elizabeth had just finished her little speech when there were three quick knocks on the door. Abruptly they stopped talking. At the passwords Big Joe unbolted the door and let Mrs. Coffin in with their supper. She sat and chatted with them while they ate. When she got up to leave, she assured them that the sheriff and the slave catchers had left the house.

But it wasn't until three days later that Mr. Coffin came to the cellar room and said it was safe for them to leave. He guided them through the dark passageway to the back of his store where a delivery wagon stood waiting. The driver motioned for them to lie down on the wagon bed behind some sacks of grain. "You'll be freight bound for a schooner docked at Cleveland," he told them. "It's all been arranged."

The kind Quaker abolitionist and his wife bade them Godspeed, and before they knew it, they were rumbling through the streets of Cincinnati to the railroad station. It was a short ride, and soon they felt the wagon slowing to a stop. After a long moment they heard their driver tell someone in a guarded voice, "Friends with a friend."

The three fugitives were hurried into a boxcar where once again they were instructed to lie quietly among the sacks of grain.

"When you get to Cleveland, a conductor of the Underground Railroad will meet you. You'll know him by the passwords, 'Friends with a friend.' " The train gave a sudden lurch at that moment, and the delivery man straightened up and quickly left the boxcar.

" 'Board! All aboard!" a voice called out along the line of cars.

Their door banged shut. With a final lurch the train for Cleveland moved slowly ahead. "We're on our way," came Elizabeth's tight voice from the pile of sacks, "an' this time we're *really* on the Underground Railroad."

They dozed off and on to the gentle sway of the boxcar and the hum of iron wheels on the tracks, waking suddenly each time the train slowed down and jerked to a stop at a station. Then they held their breath and crouched further back among the sacks as they listened for boxcar doors to be pushed open and more freight to be loaded on the train.

Day blended into night. They ate the bread and cheese Mrs. Coffin had stuffed into their sweater pockets before they left. Ben was just dozing off again when the train screeched shrilly to a stop. From down the line they could hear the doors of the boxcars being slid open.

They waited for the train to start up again, and when it didn't Big Joe whispered, "I has the feelin' we's at Cleveland."

They lay mouse-still, waiting. Ben listened anxiously when the door to their car rattled open and a voice called out, "I'm from the schooner *Erie*. Our shipment is in this car, I believe. I can load it on the wagon myself."

There were sounds of a wagon being backed up against the boxcar; then hurried footsteps sounded on the floor of the car. Seconds later a low voice whispered close to their ears, "Friends with a friend."

The sacks around them were moved from the boxcar to

93

the wagon outside. Among the sacks, Ben found himself being half-carried out of the boxcar and onto the wagon.

It was dark, and a chill drizzle swept over them. Ben shivered in the damp wagon bed as he listened to the sounds of train noises and people calling back and forth. Suddenly he stiffened when above the confusion of voices he heard a cry, "Search those boxcars for runaway slaves!"

There was the sound of running feet. The next moment the wagon springs creaked loudly as the driver leaped on the seat and grabbed the reins. In haste he called out to the horses, and they rumbled away from the station, leaving the shouts of the slave catchers dying on the night air.

A short time later the wagon jolted to a stop. Again Ben felt himself being hurried from the wagon bed into a dark, moving place. A pair of firm hands guided him past boxes and bales and casks. A voice close to his ear whispered, "You're on the *Erie* now—Captain Evans' Abolition Boat."

In the light of the lantern the man was carrying, Ben saw a face as black as his own, grinning down at him.

"Who—who are you?" he trembled.

"I'm one of Captain Evans' roustabouts, and I'm free," the black man said proudly. "There's no passengers aboard till morning, so you be safe here in the hold." Saying no more, the man disappeared into the darkness.

In the dim light of the lantern the roustabout had left, Ben saw Big Joe and Elizabeth moving toward him. A weary smile curved Elizabeth's mouth. "Just one more journey till we gets to the Promised Land Massa Parker told us about," she said.

Ben's stiff body relaxed. "Canada!" he whispered to himself. "Canada!"

For the rest of the night they slept in the hold of the *Erie* to the gentle rocking of the schooner. The clanging of a bell the next morning and the swaying of the planks beneath them told them that the *Erie* was setting sail.

"We's leavin' Cleveland," Big Joe said with a broad grin. "We's headin' straight for the Promised Land!" And no sooner were his words spoken than the schooner swung around into the wind, and they could hear the swish of its bow cutting through the water.

It was late in the day when the hatch to the hold was opened and a stout man in uniform climbed down the steps and approached them.

"Friends with a friend," he said, smiling, as they scrambled to their feet. "I am Captain Evans. We are now in Canadian waters, and I thought you would like to see Canada when it comes into view. Follow me up on deck."

Elizabeth held back. There was a thin edge of fear to her voice. "Be—be it safe?"

"It's safe," Captain Evans replied. "You are in free waters now."

A shiver of joy shot through Ben as they took hands and followed the captain up a narrow stairway and along a corridor lined with small cabin doors on either side. Finally, up another flight of stairs and they were on the open deck. They stood in the bow with the captain and looked out over the rail. The air was cool and crisp. All around them, as far as they could see, was the rolling blue water of the great Lake Erie.

Ben could hardly believe that they were free at last. It seemed strange to stand here under the open sky and not have to be afraid.

The captain pointed to the northwest. "Keep looking in that direction," he told them, "and you'll get your first sight of land. It won't be long now."

As Ben kept his eyes on the far horizon, there was a question about Canada that he had to ask, and he thought the captain would know the answer. He asked it. "Is there a school in Canada where black folks can learn to read?"

Captain Evans put his arm around the boy's shoulder. "There's a school at the mission in Amherstburg," he said. "They'll teach you to read and write and do sums."

Ben looked up at the captain and smiled the biggest smile he had ever smiled in his entire life. Then Big Joe exclaimed in an excited voice, "Captain, is that land?"

He pointed to what looked like a cloud bank along the horizon. The captain nodded. It wasn't long before they could make out trees and houses along a low flat shoreline.

Elizabeth clutched the rail tightly with her long black fingers. "Canada," she breathed in a voice that shook with emotion. "We has reached the freedom land!"

The slanting sun, a crimson disk, tinted the waves a shimmering amber. It colored the land beyond a coppery golden that reminded Ben of his good luck penny.

He could see the coin now in his mind's eye as plainly as if he were looking at it in the palm of his hand. Around the top of the penny the word Liberty, which meant freedom, stood out with bright, shiny letters. And as the shoreline of Canada drew nearer and nearer, Ben felt a happiness he had never known before. Now, for the first time in his life, he knew what those letters meant.

NANCY

1

NANCY GARDNER opened her journal and dipped her pen into a bottle of ink. In fine, flowing letters she wrote: Sims' Landing, Kentucky. May 1, 1852.

She blinked her eyes in thought for a moment, then bent her head over the blank page and began to write: Tomorrow we are finally leaving for Oregon. We are going to make our new home in the Willamette Valley, where Papa intends to take up a claim. We had heard that the land there is so fertile that it will grow just about anything, and Papa said that, as a farmer, there will be a better chance for him to get ahead in Oregon than in Kentucky.

Nancy paused thoughtfully, dipping her pen several more times in the ink. Then she continued, writing as fast as her thoughts came.

We had wanted to start out earlier for Oregon, but it took

Papa and George longer than they expected to find just the right kind of covered wagon to get us there. Papa said it couldn't be just any kind of wagon, but had to be large and sturdy to stand the long journey of twenty-five hundred miles from here to the Willamette Valley.

The wagon Papa bought is big and grand, about nine or ten feet long and about four feet wide. It has a twill top that George waterproofed with linseed oil. Six bows of bent hickory support the top, and there are flaps in the front and a puckering string in the back to let air through.

"It's like a tiny room," I said when I first climbed inside and stood upright along the center line.

"Just right to play house in with your dollies," laughed Harry, who is forever teasing me. He knows I am much too old to play with dolls. As usual I ignored him and went on inspecting the wagon that is to be our home until we reach Oregon.

All week Mama and I have been busy packing our bedding, clothes, and food that we'll need for our long journey in the covered wagon. Papa and the boys have loaded our smaller farm wagon with the plow and some goods to barter with the Indians. We call that wagon the trade wagon.

Mama is sad at having to leave so many of her precious possessions behind, but Papa said we can take only what is absolutely necessary. We even have to leave half of our clothes and sell most of our furniture. Mama gave Grandma her good rosebud china so that she wouldn't have to sell it, and that made her feel better.

At last we are packed and ready to go. Uncle Bert and Grandma are coming over tomorrow to see us off. Uncle Bert bought our farm and he, Grandma, Aunt Laura, and our three cousins will be living here at Sims' Landing after we are gone.

How I shall miss the farm and Sims' Landing! But most of all I shall miss school. Mama, who used to be a teacher, said we could take our books and slates along and she would set lessons for us. Harry didn't like that idea at all, but I gladly packed mine. Some day I'd like to be a teacher, too.

Today Nathan Johnson, who lives on the farm next to ours, came over to say good-bye. Nathan is my very best friend at Sims' Landing. We walked down to the river to our secret meeting place, the old cave in the cove.

What fun we always had playing in that old cave! We used to play river pirates and wild Indians, and once we found an Indian cook pot hidden way back on a ledge. But now that we're older, we mostly sit and talk in our cave. We can tell each other things that we can't tell our parents. It seems that older people just don't seem to understand how young people feel these days.

Well, today after I told Nathan how sad I was about leaving him, he glanced gravely into the shadows of the cave and didn't say anything for a long time. I knew he felt as sad about saying good-bye as I, but being a boy, he didn't like to admit it.

Suddenly Nathan's eyes focused on something back in the cave, and he leaned over and pulled out an old ticking bag, just like Grandma's. Only this one was such a filthy old bag that I thought maybe a tramp had left it in the cave. Nathan wondered if it may have belonged to one of those runaway slaves that Sheriff Henderson had warned us about.

"You remember, Nance, the sheriff told us to keep our eyes open for a field hand and his wife and a fourteen-year-old boy," Nathan reminded me.

I have been thinking all week about that poor slave boy, who is the same age as Nathan and I, and secretly hope that he will be able to get away from those mean-looking slave hunters and their bloodhounds. Nathan agreed, too, that if we saw the runaway slave boy, we wouldn't tell Sheriff Henderson about him.

When Nathan opened the ticking bag, he drew out a moldy hoecake, an old threadbare blanket, and a pair of boy's farm shoes. He reached to the very bottom of the bag and brought out a copper coin. He turned it over in his hand and whistled softly.

"The date on this penny goes back to 1794," he said. "Wonder where the slave boy got such an old penny? It must have been his because it came from this bag his shoes were in."

After examining the penny closely, he handed it to me and said, "Here, Nance, you take it."

"But do you think it's right to keep his penny?" I asked.

"That slave boy is probably miles away from here by now," Nathan replied, "and with Sheriff Henderson around, he won't be coming back to this cave. Anyway, it's only a penny."

"Well, you found it," I said. "Finders, keepers."

"But you're the one going away," he persisted, "so you should have it—sort of as a good luck piece."

I thought it was very nice of Nathan to give me the old penny. I told him that I would call it my good luck penny, and I would always think of him when I looked at it.

I almost cried when we had to leave the cave and it was time to say good-bye. I'm glad I didn't, though, because that would have made Nathan feel funny, and it would have made our parting all the sadder. How I shall miss him!

2

DEAR JOURNAL, you are all the friend I have now because since I left Nathan, I have nobody to share my
thoughts with. Oh, I have my family: Mama and Papa, my
little sister Carrie, my big brother George, and Harry, who is
two years older than I and an awful tease. I love them all
dearly, but a girl needs a friend outside her family to talk to,
and Nathan was such a dear friend. I wonder if he misses me
as much as I miss him.

With parting tears and good-byes, we started out from
Sims' Landing two weeks ago. We must have looked like a
little parade. Papa led the way with the big covered wagon;
George followed, driving the team of horses that pulled the

trade wagon; and Harry brought up the rear, leading our three milk cows.

Papa had a wild cherry blossom pinned to his shirt. He loves flowers, and when they are in bloom, he always has one pinned to his shirt bosom. He says it makes him feel happy to be wearing a flower. Even when he was working in our fields, he would pick a dandelion or a daisy to wear. The day we left Sims' Landing he looked especially happy wearing the wild cherry blossom.

We have four oxen pulling the big covered wagon. I have already given them names. Whitey and Alfred are the wheel oxen, and the lead oxen are Red and Puller. Whitey has a white head, and Red is the dark red ox. Puller is always pulling ahead as though to urge the other three to go faster. Alfred has no unusual characteristics, so I just named him that because I like the name.

It is now the middle of May, and we have arrived at St. Joseph, Missouri. Several days ago we crossed the Missouri River on a steamboat, and Papa had the wagons and animals ferried across on a big wooden flatboat. All up and down the western side of the river there are covered wagons and tents where people are camping while they wait to start westward. From the river the western shore looks like a big tent city.

It is warm enough now to sleep in our own tent; so we, too, are camping out while Papa and George are purchasing food and provisions in St. Joseph. They are also making arrangements for us to travel with a wagon train going to Oregon.

Yesterday while I took care of Carrie, I met a girl about my age walking with her little sister along the river. I showed her my old penny which I keep tied in a corner of my handkerchief for safekeeping. I told her it was a good luck penny, given to me by a dear friend. She said she had never seen a penny that old before. When she finished looking at it, I tied it in the corner of my handkerchief again, and for the rest of the afternoon we talked together under a weeping willow while our little sisters played.

Today my new friend is gone. In another day we will be leaving St. Joseph, too. Mama says that she regrets leaving because St. Joseph is the last civilized place we'll see for a long time. But I am glad to get away from all the noise and confusion here. It'll be good to get onto the open prairie where there will be peace and quiet again.

On the Oregon Trail
May 17, 1852

Yesterday we joined a wagon train of emigrants for Oregon. Emigrants, that's what we're called. We may not be traveling across the ocean, but we are traveling all the way across the country, and George says that's about as far.

There are fifty wagons in our train. Our guide and wagon master is an experienced voyageur who has been over the emigration road several times. He has also spent a year in the wilderness of the Rocky Mountains. Dressed in a fringed buckskin jacket and trousers, he is a wild-looking man with long black hair and very brown skin. Mama said he looks more like an Indian than a white man, but Papa has great faith in him as a guide.

Our wagons went northward along the Missouri River, and our first day's journey was only six miles. But we are now fairly embarked and things are beginning to assume the appearance of order.

Today we turned westward where the Missouri meets the North Platte River. We are following the North Platte westward on the Oregon Trail, the name of our emigration road. Mama had tears in her eyes as she glanced back and told me, "Nancy, all that we know now lies behind us—our farm, our family, our friends. There is no turning back for us now. Your Papa is determined to get to the Willamette Valley." With a sigh she added, "But, oh, what will we have to go through to get there?"

I squeezed her hand and whispered, "Papa will see that we get there all right, Mama." But as I spoke these words, I put my other hand into the pocket of my dress and held tightly the good luck penny Nathan had given me.

From the wagon seat Mama, little Carrie, and I can look out over the long line of white wagon tops. Papa walks alongside our two yoke of oxen that plod patiently along. All around us are the sounds of creaking wheels, the jangling of chain locks, and the plod of oxen feet, sounds which we will hear for many weeks to come and, I hope, will grow accustomed to.

The prairie looks beautiful this time of year. It is a perfect sea of deep flowing grass with so many pretty wildflowers— pink and white and yellow. Papa picked a flower to pin to his shirt, and I decided that when we stopped at the end of the day, I would pick some wildflowers to cheer Mama.

Today we saw Indians along our route. Most of them sat on their ponies in a line and stared at our many wagons. I wonder what thoughts lay behind those expressionless brown faces as they watch so many white people pass through their land.

3

On the Prairie

WE HAVE been traveling many days on the prairie—so many that I have lost track of them. Mama and Carrie usually ride in the wagon, but I would rather be walking on the trail like most of the young people. Sometimes I walk with Harry and the cows, when he's not teasing me, and sometimes I walk up front with Papa. The oxen go so slowly that it's not hard to keep up with the wagons. The road we are traveling is good, but at times the dust is so unbearable I find myself wandering off the trail and walking through the prairie grass which is so tall that it comes to my waist.

At the end of each day it is a relief to stop and rest my weary feet. The wagons are driven into a big circle that serves as a corral for our stock and barricades us from storms and possible Indian attacks. Mr. Ragot, our guide, told us that the Indians are usually peaceful, but now and then there have been incidents of renegade bands attacking wagon trains for the booty they can get.

The oxen are driven in the center of our wagon circle. The cattle and horses are kept in a night corral with the men taking turns guarding them. We all have our chores to do at the end of the day. Papa and the boys put up our tent and feed and water the stock while Mama and I cook supper over an open fire. We have eaten all our fresh meat, but we still have bacon, salt pork, and plenty of cornmeal. When wood is scarce, we gather buffalo chips that burn as clean and as well as dry wood. While walking along the trail during the day, it is my chore to gather buffalo chips for our fire at night.

There are several fiddlers in our wagon train, and often there is fiddling, singing, and storytelling around the campfire. Each night, before we go to bed, Papa reads a chapter from our big family Bible, and more than anything else those holy words give us comfort.

Often we meet bands of Indians along the trail. The men are tall and proud and usually refuse the presents we offer them, but the Indian women, with babies tied to cradleboards on their backs, gladly take the gifts. They are very fond of white children, and we've heard stories of Indians wanting to adopt them.

One day a squaw stepped up to our wagon to touch Carrie's yellow curls. Poor Mama! She did not want to offend the Indian woman, but she held Carrie tightly in her arms. Later she told us that she was afraid the Indians would steal her little girl.

Day after day passes. Sometimes I wonder if we'll ever come to our journey's end. We are well into summer now, but Papa said it won't be until October when we reach the Willamette Valley. It seems as though I have been traveling in a covered wagon all my life.

At first it was fun to walk the trail and to camp out every night, but now even George and Harry admit that it would be good to sit down at a table for a meal and to sleep in a real bed again.

We are meeting more and more wagons passing us on their way back East. When I was riding in the trade wagon with George, I asked him why so many wagons are turning back.

"Because they are afraid of the cholera," George told me. "It's a terrible sickness, Nancy."

The green prairie has been long behind us, and now we see nothing but sagebrush. The heat and the dust and the mosquitoes are getting unbearable, but Papa said that we shouldn't complain when so many of our fellow travelers are coming down with the sickness and we are still well and able to travel.

Every day now we see fresh mounds along the trail that are the graves of the victims of the dreaded cholera. Many wagons in our train are turning back, but in the midst of all this Papa tries his best to keep up our courage, and like a good shepherd he continues to guide his little flock steadily onward.

On Sundays, a day of rest from the weary traveling, we hold a simple service in our tent. Now and then itinerant preachers will stop and hold services for all the emigrants of our wagon train. Then Papa will put on his linsey coat, and George and Henry their good butternut jeans tucked into their high leather boots. Mama, Carrie, and I will wear our dark calico dresses and new gingham sunbonnets. Sedately we follow Papa to one of the bigger tents where the service is heid. Mama always enjoys these Sunday meetings. She says they bring home a little closer to us out here in the wilderness.

One day when the rain fell in torrents, Carrie came down with the sickness. She complained that her head ached and she lay listlessly in Mama's lap all morning. By afternoon she said her stomach hurt and she kept vomiting and asking for water. Mama put a warm flannel cloth across her stomach, but Carrie kept complaining that she hurt all over.

When the wagons stopped for the night, Papa went for a doctor who is going west with our wagon train. The poor man looked gray and weary as he caught hold of the wagon bed and mounted the wheel spokes to climb into our wagon. There was so much sickness, he said, that he had no time to sleep.

We hoped that Carrie had just an upset stomach, but when the doctor said that it was the cholera, our hearts fell. He told us to be sure to boil our drinking water and to keep Carrie warm. Beyond that there was nothing much he could do because all his medicines were gone.

Mama and I took turns sitting up with poor Carrie that night. She would toss and whimper pitifully, then would sink into a restless slumber, only to awaken to more tossing and whimpering. Three days later while I was sitting with her in the hot, jolting wagon, her whimpering stopped and she lay white and still.

That late afternoon when we stopped, Papa dug a little grave in the shelter of some cottonwood trees and said a simple service for her. Before he left Carrie's grave, he unpinned the wilted lupine he wore on his shirt and laid it tenderly on the little mound.

All night Mama sat by Carrie's grave, and when morning

came and it was time for the wagons to leave, she refused to move. Papa had to carry her to the wagon seat.

All that day Mama did not shed a tear but kept staring blankly ahead of her as if she were in some kind of trance. It wasn't until that night when Papa took the Bible from the wagon and read the Twenty-third Psalm that the tears finally came to her eyes.

"Yea, though I walk through the valley of the shadow of death, I will fear no evil," Papa read in his strong but gentle voice, "for thou art with me; thy rod and thy staff they comfort me."

I think about those words often as I walk alongside our wagon, and whenever we pass new, small mounds along the trail that remind me of our poor little Carrie, those words bring me comfort.

4

Fort Hall

WE HAVE reached Fort Hall and have been camping here for several days. The front axle of the trade wagon gave way, and Papa has to have it repaired by the blacksmith. There is quite a line of wagons waiting to be repaired, and Papa says we will just have to be patient and wait our turn.

Mama and I washed all our clothes, and we were able to buy some flour at the fort to bake with, although it is very expensive. Now that all our work is done, I decided that this is a good time to catch up on my writing. When we are on the trail, I cannot write with the jolting of the wagon, and when we stop at night, I am usually too tired. So while we wait for the trade wagon to be repaired, I shall bring you up to date, dear journal.

So much has happened since I last wrote in you that I hardly know where to begin. After our poor little Carrie died, Mama was feeling so poorly that I wanted to help her as much as I could; so I was busy from morn till night, cooking and keeping the wagon tidy. But now, even though Mama still looks pale and there are tiny lines of sadness around her eyes, she is able to smile again, for which we are all thankful.

Our wagon train is only half the size it was when we started out from St. Joseph in the spring. So many emigrants have come down with the cholera or have lost heart and turned back. The ones of us who remain are like one big family now, sharing one another's hardships and helping out whenever we can.

One day from across the flat plains we caught sight of high mountain peaks in the distance. Papa said they were the Rocky Mountains. I thought they were well named because they were nothing but huge rock heaped upon rock. They were so high that the peaks were covered with snow. Quite pretty in the sunset.

The passage through these mountains was in a valley. It was so gradual an ascent that I should not have known we were crossing the Rockies until Papa told us. The air was cold and fresh, but it was thin and we all tired easily.

When we stopped for the night at South Pass, the summit of the Rocky Mountains, George pointed to the peaks to the north and cried, "Look at that sight!"

"They are the Wind River Mountains," Mr. Ragot informed us, "and a prettier sight you won't see in a long time." He told us that we were now drinking water from streams that flowed to the Pacific. Harry gave an exulted whoop and I joined him. What an achievement to have made it this far!

After we left South Pass, Mr. Ragot called a meeting to decide which way to take. He told the men that the Oregon Trail dipped southward to Fort Bridger, but that there was a shorter way called Sublette's Cutoff, which would save us a day or two of travel. The cutoff was through the desert, he warned, and it was wild country. But the men decided that we had enough water to see us across and cutting a day or two of travel heartened them. Everyone is eager to get to Oregon before the early winter sets in.

Several days later we started across Sublette's Cutoff, forty-one miles without water. Mama said she had never known a place that could be so hot and dry. She stayed in the wagon while I walked alongside the oxen with Papa. Soon my feet were burning on the white dust that covered the ground, and I ran to the wagon for my shoes. Papa said the dust was alkali. It was everywhere, glistening like fine powdered snow. There were dry lake beds of it, crusted hard and thick, and whole stretches of white flats spread out before us.

The oxen dropped their heads but kept plodding patiently on, even though their feet were tender and bleeding from the hot desert floor. My own feet were burning through the shoe leather. I longed to ride in the wagon, but I didn't have the heart to add more weight for the oxen to pull. Besides, I didn't want to give old Harry the opportunity of saying that a girl can't walk across the desert as well as a boy.

We were all relieved when Mr. Ragot called for an early stop. We camped in a wild, beautiful place with ragged mountains close to the north of us. There was no fuel for our cooking fires, not even buffalo chips, so Mama and the other women laid out pots of cold baked beans, cold biscuits, and dried apple pies for supper. We all sat down to a cold meal, but nobody cared after the scorching heat of the day.

It was after supper, when I was helping Harry bed down the cows, that we heard the sudden thudding of horses' hoofs across the dry flats. A moment later there were high shrill yells and hideous shrieks all around us.

"What is it? What is it?" cried voices around the circle of wagons.

Then someone screamed, "Indians!"

Next I could distinguish Mr. Ragot's voice calling: "A raiding party. We're being ambushed."

Harry shouted excitedly and pointed to about a dozen Indians riding into our camp. They had slashes of red and yellow paint across their brown faces and eagle feathers in their black hair. The fringes of their buckskins were flying as they galloped around us.

We were all taken by surprise and were totally unprepared for such an attack. Men, women, and children were running in all directions, and there was confusion everywhere. Papa called for Harry and me to run to the wagon where Mama was. George dashed ahead of us to the trade wagon for his flintlock.

In my haste I tripped over a rock and fell flat on the desert floor. As I was getting to my feet, a painted Indian leaned down from his pony and grabbed me, swinging me up in front of him on his horse. It had all happened so suddenly and I was so stunned by fright that by the time I came to my senses and could call for help, my captor was galloping across the plain toward the mountains.

I struggled to free myself, but the Indian held me fast, at the same time urging his swift pony up a steep trail that wound between rock ledges. Soon we were hidden by high rocky bluffs, but we could still hear those terrible Indian shrieks from the desert below.

As we climbed higher into the mountains, the sounds

faded away in the distance, and I felt a sick feeling in the pit of my stomach. Would I ever see the wagon train again? I wondered.

We kept riding on a trail that I thought was impossible to climb. It was so narrow and steep that it seemed to go up the sheer face of a cliff. But the Indian pony was surefooted, and my captor seemed to know the trail well.

In time we reached a plateau at the top of the cliff which was dotted with several tepees made of animal skins. In the center of the tepees was a cooking fire, and around it sat several squaws. This must be the raiders' camp, I thought.

The Indian swung down from his pony and lifted me to the ground. He beckoned to one of the women who came to meet me. She was uglier and older than the other squaws— in fact, she was the ugliest woman I had ever seen. She pushed me toward the fire and pointed to the ground. I guessed that she wanted me to sit with her by the fire, so I obeyed her orders.

Gradually my numbness left me, and thoughts of my wretched fate filled my mind. Tears came into my eyes and I gave a little sob. I was reaching into the pocket of my dress for my handkerchief when my fingers touched the copper penny tied in a corner of it.

At least, I thought, I have one thing from home, and I hugged the penny against my wet cheek. At that moment it was the most precious thing I had ever had.

The Indian woman leaned over a kettle that hung above the fire and ladled some stew into a pewter bowl that had probably belonged to an emigrant woman going west. I wondered what booty besides myself the outlaw band would get from our wagons.

When the bowl was handed to me, I shook my head. I could not eat the unappetizing food and pushed the bowl away. The woman's dark, ugly face showed quick anger. She kept insisting that I eat. Fearing for my life, I managed to gulp down a mouthful of the tasteless food, which seemed to please her.

The other women drew close to me and touched my long blond hair with their greasy fingers. They made low murmuring noises as women do when admiring something strange and wonderful.

It was almost dark when the raiding party returned to camp. I recognized the sack of trade goods Mr. Ragot gives to the Indians along the way in return for fresh meat. Other than the trade goods, several horses, and myself, they had little to show for their attack on our wagons.

Through frightened eyes I noticed that one of the raiders was a boy no older than Harry. He stood back from the others who were greedily pulling things out of the sack of trade goods. He was dressed in a blue calico shirt, leather pants, and a beaded headband that held back his long black hair. Slung over his shoulder was a bag made of buffalo skin. He seemed to have no interest in his share of the trade goods but kept looking at me with his dark intense eyes until I felt uneasy and turned mine away.

After a while a tall Indian wearing a gaudy shirt and brass bands around his wrists came over to me. He seemed to be the leader of the band. With him was the youth who had been staring at me. In a mixture of grunts and syllables, the leader spoke to the boy, then pointed to me. The boy said, "You, white girl, our captive."

I was relieved that one of them could speak English, and I answered quickly, "You can't keep me here. The men from the wagons won't let you. My father and brothers will come after me."

The boy repeated what I had said to the leader who

frowned and grunted some scornful sounds. The boy turned to me again and said, "White men cannot find our camp at night. By sunup we will be gone."

After muttering a few syllables to the ugly squaw, the leader walked away with the boy. The woman jerked me to my feet and beckoned. I followed her to one of the tepees where she pushed me inside under the low flap. She did not follow me in but sat outside as if to guard the entrance so that I could not escape.

When my eyes became accustomed to the dim interior, I spied a buffalo robe spread out on the ground in the back of the tent. As I sank down on the rough fur, a rush of fear and loneliness came over me. What would become of me as a captive of the Indians? I wondered. Would I be forced to become one of them, never to see my family or other white people again?

Tears streamed down my cheeks and I cried for a long time. At last, too weary to weep one more tear, I lay back on the buffalo robe, holding the handkerchief and penny tightly in my hand for comfort.

I could not sleep. Even after the Indians were quiet and the campfire flickered down to bright embers, I could not sleep. Troubled thoughts kept racing around in my mind. I could picture Mama, tearful at losing another child. I could see Papa's stern, sad face, George's angry one, and Harry's frightened look. I knew that Papa and the men in the wagon train would search for me, but how could they find me, I thought, if the Indians would be leaving at sunup?

Out of desperation thoughts of escape filled my mind. Maybe I could slip past the old squaw, who now lay sound asleep just inside the entrance of the tepee. Maybe I could make my way, unnoticed, out of the Indian camp.

But my hopes died as reason returned to my thoughts.

Even if I were able to escape from the Indian camp, where would I go? How could I find my way back to the wagons? I could never make my way down that steep, treacherous mountain trail alone at night.

Discouraged and more frightened than ever, I sank back on the buffalo robe. I was so distraught that I had forgotten my prayers, and all I could think of to say was simply, "Please, God, let me get back to the wagon train."

In spite of everything my weary body ached for sleep, and after a while I found myself dozing off. At first I thought I was dreaming when I heard a small sound on the wall of the tepee just beside my head. But when the scratching sound came again, my eyes flew wide open. Was it some kind of animal trying to get inside? I wondered.

Curiously I lifted my head, then caught my breath. There, against the wall of the tent, was a dark shadow. But it was not the shadow of an animal; it was the shadow of a crouched human being. The next moment I heard a voice warn softly, "White girl, keep quiet."

I knew that voice at once. It belonged to the Indian youth who had stared at me across the campfire. It was the same voice that had spoken for the leader. What was the Indian boy doing here, at this time of night? I wondered.

Then to my surprise, I saw something move at the ground below the edge of the tepee, and I could make out a hand. With a soft grunt, the Indian boy lifted the taut skin side upward and peered in at me. His voice whispered close to my ear, "White girl, follow."

He beckoned for me to slide under the edge of the tepee which he held open as wide as he could. Inch by inch I slid through the narrow opening. A stone rattled under my knee as I was wriggling through, and I held my breath, not daring to move farther until I was sure the Indian woman who guarded the entrance had not heard. Her sleeping form didn't move, and the boy urged me to get to my feet and to follow quickly.

We crept past the glowing embers of the campfire and skirted the backs of the other tents. At the far side of the plateau, the boy motioned for me to wait in the shadows while he slipped quietly into a rocky enclosure where the horses were tethered. He scarcely made a sound as he backed a spotted pony away from the others and led it to where I was standing. In one silent motion he leaped upon the pony's back and gave me a hand up behind him. The next moment we were off, down the same trail which I had come up only hours before.

The steep trail was scarcely visible in the starlight, but the youth seemed to know the way as well by night as by day. Now and then he would pull the pony up short and pause to listen if we were being followed. But the night hung like a dark silent curtain around us.

As we made our way down the steep mountain, I asked him where he was taking me, and he told me back to the wagons. My joy knew no bounds, but at the same time I was puzzled by his actions. I knew the Indian band would be furious with him if they knew he had let their white captive escape.

"Why are you helping me?" I asked.

"I was once a captive myself," he replied solemnly. "I belong to the Nez Percé tribe, far to the west. The Blackfoot tribe raided my village. They brought me to their country. A Blackfoot chief adopted me as his son." He paused a moment, then added, "I know how white girl felt. I saw fear and great sadness in her eyes across the fire."

I was very grateful to my rescuer, but I was still curious about him. "How did you learn to speak English?" I asked.

120

I could feel his back stiffen proudly. "I am Running Bear, son of a chief," he replied. "A white trader taught my father and me how to talk the language of the White Man."

"Running Bear," I said softly. "That's a very nice name. My name is Nancy."

"Nancee," he pronounced awkwardly but tenderly.

We rode the rest of the way down the dark trail in silence. When we reached the bottom, Running Bear sent his pony in a gallop across the desert plain. He rode low, clinging to the animal's neck. I bent my body over his and hung on to him for dear life.

When the dark outlines of the wagons came into view, he pulled his pony to a sliding stop, leaped off, and helped me down. He pointed to the wagons, and my heart leaped for joy at seeing our camp.

"Nancee, go now," the Indian youth said, and his voice had an urgency in it that told me he was anxious to be off to his own camp before dawn broke and he was missed. But before he mounted his pony, he reached into the buffalo skin bag that he still had slung across his shoulder and brought out a short string of colored Indian beads which he handed me.

I stared in wonder at the gift and knew it meant that I should hold no hard feelings for my captors. I wished with all my heart that I had a gift to give to him in return for my rescue, but I had nothing except my good luck penny, safe in the pocket of my dress.

I paused, uncertainly, for a long moment; then slowly I brought out the handkerchief and untied the knot in the corner of it.

"This is all I can give you," I said as I handed the coin to him. "It is only a penny and not worth much, but it is my good luck penny. Maybe it will bring you good luck, too."

He glanced down at the penny as if it were a gold coin. Clutching it in his hand, he swung up on his mount and without saying another word, he was off across the plain. I watched until he and his pony blended into the shadows of the night, then joyfully I made my way on foot to the wagon train.

5

Along the Snake River

YESTERDAY we left Fort Hall. Papa and the boys are glad
to be on our way again, but looking back at the fort, with its
whitewashed walls, its gardens and cornfield, Mama and I
were a little reluctant to say good-bye.

The plain we are crossing is level and follows the Snake
River. Unlike the muddy Platte, the Snake River is filled
with ripples of white water and has many springs to feed it.
We no longer have to worry about a water supply for our-
selves or for the stock.

A cool breeze made the day quite pleasant. At night we
camped along the river and had a good supper from the food
we had purchased at the fort.

After my capture by the Blackfeet, I have been staying

close to the wagons at all times, and whenever we pass Indians on the trail, I find myself scurrying up into our covered wagon and staying there until they are out of sight. I still have the fear of a painted face appearing suddenly out of nowhere and strong arms grabbing me up on an Indian pony. Papa said it will be a long time before I overcome that fear.

Harry asks over and over again to tell him about my experiences in the Blackfoot camp. He says he wishes we would come across Running Bear sometime so that he could thank him properly for helping his sister escape. Harry is really a dear and loving brother, even though he is such a tease. I think now he is proud to have a sister who was captured by the Indians.

I often wonder about my penny and the adventures it is having with Running Bear. I hope it brought him good luck and that he got back to the Blackfoot camp before the Indians discovered I was missing. I giggle to myself every time I imagine the expression on that ugly old squaw's face when she found the tepee empty the next morning.

About the penny—I am glad I gave it to Running Bear, but I miss it sorely. Every time I reach into the pocket of my dress for my handkerchief and find it unknotted, I feel a lump in my throat. My good luck penny was such a comfort to me on this long, hard journey. I wonder what Nathan would think if he knew that I had given it to an Indian. But I'm sure he'd say that I did right.

The Dalles

We are now in Oregon, dear journal! It is October and the birches and beeches are a bright yellow, and the hardwoods flame red and golden against dark stands of fir and pine.

124

We have been following the Columbia River, and today we reached a place called The Dalles. Here the great river is nearly choked by a series of falls and cataracts and by masses of black treacherous rock. Never before have I seen such a wild but beautiful scene. High cliffs frame the banks on either side and as I gaze at this strange scenery, I wonder if we are still on this earth or if, by chance, we had been transported to another planet.

At The Dalles our wagon train broke up, and we said good-bye to Mr. Ragot, who will be guiding another expedition into Canada. Now we are on our own, each family going its separate way. Some emigrants are staying at The Dalles; some are going down the Columbia River by flatboat to Fort Vancouver. Our destination is across the Cascade Mountains to Oregon City in the Willamette Valley.

There is a military post here at The Dalles. While Papa and the boys went to the post to see about the route across the Cascades, Mama and I washed our clothes and used the flatirons for the first time in many months.

When Papa and the boys returned from the fort, Harry ran ahead to be the first one to tell us the news. He said that the officer in command was a very kind and helpful gentleman who offered to send a yoke of oxen and two men to see our wagons to the summit. Harry said the officer's name was Captain Ulysses S. Grant and that he came from Ohio.

The Willamette Valley

It took us over a week to cross the Cascades. The journey was a hard one, and many times we all had to leave the wagons and walk. I pitied the poor oxen that had to strain and pull the big wagons through those steep, rugged passes.

Often I walked alongside them, calling them each by name and patting their huge, sweaty bodies to encourage them along.

At the summit we bid good-bye to Captain Grant's men and thanked them heartily. I don't know how we could have climbed the mountains without their help.

It was cool and pleasant on the summit, so we camped and rested for a day. As we looked westward toward the setting sun that first night, it seemed to us all, weary as we were, that the rest of the way must be downhill.

On the afternoon of the tenth day after leaving The Dalles, we saw through the trees a beautiful open valley, sprinkled with oaks and wildflowers and fringed with snow-crowned mountains stretching into the blue sky above.

"There is our valley, the end of our journey," Papa said.

Mama nodded and there were tears of joy in her eyes. "Yes, this is the Oregon I prayed we would reach—our new home."

After six long months of traveling, we have reached our destination at last. We are thin and weary, and our clothes are dirty and tattered. But Papa still has a flower pinned to the bosom of his shirt.

He stepped in front of the oxen and waved his arms back and forth to stop them. Then he gathered us all in the wagon for a prayer of thanksgiving to God. He ended his prayer with Psalm 100, and we said it with him.

"Enter into his gates with thanksgiving, and into his courts with praise; be thankful unto him, and bless his name. For the Lord is good; his mercy is everlasting; and his truth endureth to all generations."

The next day we found our way up the Willamette River in the heart of this beautiful valley where Papa decided to purchase a claim. The valley is as fertile as it is beautiful, and

126

we all agreed that it is a wonderful place for a home.

With the help of our friendly neighbors, Papa and the boys built a cabin of split boards and shingles, with a mud and stick chimney. Now they plan to break twenty acres of land and sow it with wheat. By next year we hope to have a corn patch, a vegetable garden, and an orchard. Our oxen and cows are thriving without care on the lush grass of the meadows, and soon we hope to have chickens and pigs.

Mama is so happy to have a home of her own again that she looks upon our simple cabin as a wonder. Papa laughs and says that no lady of high degree could be so happy in her castle as is our dear, brave mama in her own cabin.

Yesterday I wrote my first letter to Nathan, and Papa took it to Oregon City to mail. I like to imagine that I am that letter, traveling back across all those miles to Sims' Landing, Kentucky, and I can hardly wait for Nathan's reply to get here.

Maybe someday when the railroad crosses the continent, he will come to Oregon to visit us. Then we can talk together like old times, and I can tell him about our journey across the country and my adventures in the Blackfoot camp. And I won't forget to mention how the old penny he found in the cave and gave to me before we said good-bye proved to be a good luck penny after all.

Nancy closed her journal and laid her hand gently on the faded leather cover. "You have been a dear friend all the way across the Oregon Trail, and I have told you all my innermost thoughts," she said with a loving smile. She put the journal and pen in the drawer of the new pine nightstand her father had made for her, then she hurried down the ladder from the cabin loft to join her family by the fireside.

RUNNING BEAR

1

WINTER RAIN drummed against the taut buffalo hide of the Blackfoot tepee. It splashed in puddles by the door flap, sending a muddy trickle across the earthen floor of the dwelling. The old chief watched the rivulet as it zigzagged across the ground toward where he was sitting. He shivered and pulled his blanket tighter around his bony shoulders.

Running Bear felt sadness in his heart as he watched his father. He could remember when the Blackfoot chief was a tall, proud warrior, but now he had grown old beyond his years as he sat wrinkled and bent before his adopted son.

The chief bowed his head and his voice was bleak. "My son, I am asking you to return to the land of your people, the Nez Percés. A man should be close to the land where the bones of his ancestors are sacred and their resting place is hallowed ground."

131

"But my father," Running Bear protested, "my home is now with you. I can never leave you."

The old chief sighed. "Our people are ever fleeing the coming of the white man, as the birds flee the coming of the winter wind. The greatness of our tribe will soon be a mournful memory, and footsteps upon the land will be only echoes. I can no longer offer you the good life, my son. Flee as the birds to the land of your ancestors."

It was shortly after these words were spoken that the old chief died. When the winter rains ceased and early spring began to color the plains, Running Bear took up the buffalo skin medicine bundle that his Blackfoot mother had made for him. He opened it to see that his most precious possessions, the herbs, roots, and buffalo stones, were still there. At the bottom of the medicine bundle was a small leather pouch. He opened the pouch and drew out his amulet—his charm against evils. It was the good luck penny Nancee had given him many long years ago. He looked at the penny for a long time, then put it back in the pouch and closed his medicine bundle. Slinging it over his shoulder, he mounted his spotted pony and turned its head toward the land of the Nez Percés.

For many days he rode into the setting sun until he reached the Land of the Winding Waters in the beautiful Wallowa Valley in northeastern Oregon. There, guarded by the Bitterroot Mountains and bound by sparkling rivers, the land of his ancestors was as he remembered it in his boyhood—so many long winters ago. The grassy hills, the groves of pine, cottonwood, and fir, and the ravines filled with wild roses and chokecherry were all so familiar. The meadows ablaze with blue bells, yellow lupine, and purple shooting stars greeted him in bright array that warm spring day. With a heart filled with longing, he rode toward the

132

village by the Grande Ronde River. He was home at last.

In the village he found the same gentle, peaceful people he had remembered. When Joseph, the Nez Percé chief, heard about the return of the long lost boy, now grown to manhood, he summoned Running Bear to his lodge. He remembered Running Bear as his special boyhood friend and smiled at the thought of how they used to sail wood chips together on the river. He welcomed Running Bear back to his people and ordered the women to prepare a feast in honor of his long lost friend.

For six happy years Running Bear lived in the Wallowa Valley with the Nez Percés. But the happy days did not last. One spring morning, in 1877, some bluecoat American soldiers rode into Chief Joseph's village. Running Bear saw them from the top of the valley where he had been hunting. When he returned to the village, the soldiers were gone, and he found Joseph sitting alone in the council lodge.

"What did the bluecoats want?" he asked his friend.

"They brought news from the Grandfather in Washington," Joseph replied with a worried frown. "The Federal Government wants the Wallowa Valley for its people to settle on. We are to be confined to the Lapwai reservation with the other Nez Percé bands."

Running Bear felt his heart racing. "What will we do?" he asked. "Will we have to fight?"

Joseph shook his head. "I am a man of peace, Running Bear. My father and I never fought the White Man. Tomorrow I will meet the soldiers at Fort Lapwai. I will talk to the white war-chief, General Howard."

In the early morning Joseph set out for Fort Lapwai. His scalp lock was tied with otter fur and his long hair hung in two thick braids across his big chest. His fringed shirt and leggings had been rubbed white, and he had on his best

133

moccasins. Before he had left his lodge, his wife had hung a gray woolen shawl over his broad shoulders.

It was a beautiful May morning, and the meadows were alive with spring flowers. On such a morning Running Bear should have felt happy, but a strange anxiety hung over him as he rode beside his silent friend.

General Howard and Colonel Perry met them at the council tent on the edge of the parade ground. There Joseph, chief of the Wallowa band, joined the chiefs of the other Nez Percé bands. There was old Too-hul-hul-sote, chief of the Snake River and Seven Devils country; Looking Glass, whose band lived on the Middle Fork of the Clearwater; and Yellow Bull. White Bird, chief of the White Bird Creek band, was late, but General Howard started the council meeting without him.

"I say this to you," the stout, full-bearded general told the Nez Percés. "You must come to the reservation with your people. You must leave the Wallowa. You must obey the government of the United States in Washington."

Old Too-hul-hul-sote, a Dreamer priest and an orator, arose and stood before the general. "The Great Spirit Chief made the world as it is and as he wanted it, and he made a part of it for us to live upon," Too-hul-hul-sote said in his deep voice. "I do not see where you get authority to say that we shall not live where he placed us."

General Howard replied, "I do not care about your Great Spirit Chief. I am telling you what must be done."

Now Joseph arose and stood beside the old chief. He stood with great calmness and dignity. "We are all sprung from the Great Spirit, although we are unlike in many things," Joseph said evenly. "Then why should children of one mother and one father quarrel? Why should one try to cheat the other? I do not believe that the Great Spirit gave

134

one kind of men the right to tell another kind of men what they must do."

General Howard spoke up sharply, "You deny my authority, do you?"

Too-hul-hul-sote answered the question with angry scorn. "Are you the Great Spirit? Did you make the world? Did you make the sun? Did you make the rivers to run for us to drink and the grass to grow? Did you make all these things that you can talk to us as though we were boys? If you did, then you have the right to talk as you do."

General Howard's face turned red under his beard and his eyes flashed from beneath their bushy brows. "Are you questioning the authority of the government at Washington?"

"Is Washington the Great Spirit?" Too-hul-hul-sote said. "Did Washington make the world?"

The general arose. Turning to Colonel Perry, he roared, "I don't want to hear any more such talk. Put this impudent fellow in the guardhouse for a few days." Then turning back to the other Nez Percé chiefs, he said, "Your Great Spirit will not stop me from carrying out my orders. Your bands will leave the Wallowa. If you do not leave peacefully within thirty days, my soldiers will drive you out. These are my orders."

When Joseph and Running Bear returned to the village and told Ollicut, Joseph's brother, what General Howard had said, Ollicut exclaimed angrily, "Hai-yai! Then we will go to war!"

Joseph shook his head. "I do not want war. We have always lived in peace with the White Man."

"But now you will have to fight!" Ollicut said.

Joseph replied calmly, "They are many and we are few. If we were to go to war, we would all perish before the blue-

135

coats' guns. There is only one thing we can do to survive. We will round up our horse herds and livestock and prepare to leave for the Lapwai reservation."

The chiefs of the other bands recognized Joseph's wisdom and agreed with him. They elected Joseph, the calm and wise one, their leader for the journey to the reservation. After herding their fine Apaloosa horses and gathering provisions to take with them, the Nez Percé bands were ready to leave.

Before crossing the Snake River, Running Bear and Joseph looked back at the beautiful Land of the Winding Waters with its shining streams and slanting meadows, blue with the tops of camas.

"The land of our ancestors is no longer ours," Joseph said sadly. Then he turned his horse quickly and followed the others to the riverbank.

The Snake River was running high with the spring rains. First the range horses had to be driven across, then the people had to be taken across with their supply of food: smoked salmon, camas cakes, and pemmican. All the lodge skins and buffalo robes and other household necessities followed, tightly lashed on rafts.

It was a difficult crossing. The yellow roaring river swirled through rocky gorges and the rafts turned and tossed in the rapid waters, but at last all were safely on the eastern shore.

The people rode eastward to the Salmon River Canyon where they had another stream to cross. Again the crossing was difficult because of the swirling, swollen waters. It had taken the Nez Percé bands twenty days to cross both rivers. Now they were within two miles of the reservation.

Joseph called for a rest at White Bird Canyon. The men built brush huts against the hot June sun, and the women opened and spread out their packs to dry.

"Let us enjoy our last ten days of freedom," Joseph told his people. "We will have dances and games."

Drums began to beat, and storytellers told the legends of the tribe to the children. But the young men were restless, and this worried Joseph. He knew that they wanted to make war with the bluecoats.

But to Joseph this was not the way of the Nez Percé. Peace was the only way.

2

RUNNING BEAR was returning from a hunt two days later when he saw Little Runner, Joseph's messenger, riding out of the mouth of White Bird Canyon. He was riding hard toward Joseph's camp. Running Bear urged his mount down the canyon rim to meet the scout.

With breathless words Little Runner told him that a band of young warriors had gone up the canyon. "Shots have already been exchanged between our braves and the bluecoat scouts," Little Runner said. "Colonel Perry and a hundred cavalrymen are riding into the canyon. I have seen the sun gleam brightly on the bugle carried by the advance party."

When Joseph heard the news, he said, "It may still not be too late to try for peace." He ordered Little Runner to ride up to the cavalry with a white flag.

Little Runner swung his spotted pony around, and with

the flag snapping in the wind he galloped toward the blue-coats, but the soldiers ignored the flag of peace and fired into the canyon. Flinging the flag down, Little Runner galloped off to join the warriors.

At the end of the day the young men rode into camp with victory shouts on their lips. They had driven the bluecoats out of the canyon and back to Grangeville. "We have won our battle," they shouted proudly.

But Joseph shook his head in silence, and Running Bear knew what he was thinking. This was not the end of the battle; they had won nothing but General Howard's wrath.

Now that they had a taste of victory, the young men would not go peacefully to the reservation, and Joseph knew they could not return to the Wallowa. The only way left for the Nez Percés was the way of flight.

"We will travel the trail east to the buffalo country," Joseph told his people. "There we may be able to settle in peace."

They rode out of White Bird Canyon and started across the prairie. After many days of traveling, they stopped to rest and to gather food. The hunters shot deer and elk in the hills while the women and children dug camas roots on the prairie. Roasted in the fire, fresh camas roots tasted like sweet potatoes. It was a favorite food of the Nez Percé.

Their rest was a short one. The scouts Joseph had sent out to spy on the bluecoats came galloping back to report that General Howard's soldiers had found their camp. Joseph ordered his people to take flight at once. He knew that General Howard and Colonel Perry would not rest until the Nez Percés were on the reservation. The only hope was to escape and get to the buffalo country.

The bands crossed the Clearwater and headed toward the Bitterroot Range where the Lolo Trail led into Montana.

The trail was steep and rough, climbing ridge after ridge in the wildest wilderness. It was a hard journey for the old ones who had to be tied to travois and dragged through the hills.

June blended into July and still they climbed, hoping to elude the bluecoat general and his colonel in the mountains. They were now above the timberline in the high hills of rock and stunted pine. Clouds swirled over the mountaintops and cold rains came often. At night Running Bear listened to the coughs and the moanings of the old ones and the crying of the sick children. Still they pushed on, more and more of the sick and old ones dying. The Lolo became a trail of tears.

It was a relief to everyone when the trail finally came out to a high meadow where they could camp and rest. The hunters brought back buffalo meat from the east, and the people feasted and grew stronger. As they were about to start out again, Little Runner rode into camp with news.

"The bluecoats are ahead of us," he reported. "They are blocking our way to the Bitterroot Valley."

"How can that be?" Ollicut asked, puzzled. "We were ahead of General Howard's soldiers when we started up the Lolo Trail."

"The singing wires must have carried the general's orders to the soldiers in Montana," Joseph explained. "The singing wires can send messages many miles away."

"What are the singing wires, my father?" Joseph's twelve-year-old daughter, Sarah, asked.

Joseph looked down at her tenderly. He was very fond of his daughter and always took time to answer her questions, no matter how worried or how busy he was.

"The white men call the wires telegraph," he told her. "They are strung high above the ground on poles. They sing messages over great distances."

"How fast do the messages travel?" Sarah asked.

"Faster than a horse can gallop," her father replied. "We can never outrun them."

"The singing wires give the bluecoats strong medicine," Ollicut told his niece. Then to Joseph he asked, "What will we do?"

"We will talk," Joseph replied. "There is no reason why the Montana soldiers should block our way. We have done nothing against them."

The next day Joseph, White Bird, and Looking Glass rode up the trail to talk with the bluecoats from Montana. The three chiefs returned late the next night. They had told the bluecoat captain that they wanted a peaceful passage through the Bitterroot Valley to the buffalo country, but the captain had told them that his orders were to disarm them and to take their fine horses.

"How can we hunt the buffalo without our horses and guns?" old Too-hul-hul-sote cried, outraged.

"It is a scheme to strip us down to nothing so they can control us," White Bird muttered.

"We will not give up our horses or guns," Joseph said firmly.

"Then how will we get off this mountain?" Ollicut asked.

"I know a way," Running Bear spoke up. He turned to Joseph. "While you were gone, I found an old trail that goes up the mountain to the top where it meets a back trail to the Bitterroot Valley. If we can get the travois to the top of the mountain, we can get to the valley without continuing on this trail."

"We will get the travois up the mountain," Joseph said, reaching out and touching Running Bear's shoulder. "You have done well, old friend."

With the tent poles lashed to the horses and the travois roped in place, the bands started the steep climb up the

141

mountain the next day. Little Runner and his scouts went ahead to scout out the territory, and Joseph and Running Bear rode right behind them. High up on a cliff they stopped their spotted ponies and looked down at the camp of soldiers. Running Bear saw the sentry glance up with surprise and run to call the captain, but it did little good. Joseph's people were too far up the mountain to attack.

Running Bear and Joseph laughed heartily as they turned their horses and rode on. It felt good to be laughing at the bluecoats instead of running from them.

When they reached the summit, they stopped to wait for the others. They listened for sounds on the trail behind them, but only the shrill cry of an eagle broke the still air. Running Bear watched the great bird soar proud and free in the open sky and thought about the word "Liberty" on the copper coin Nancee had given him. He wondered if he and the Nez Percé bands would ever be free again like the eagle.

At last the others reached the summit and they crossed the Bitterroot Valley. They did not stop to rest, even though the people were weary after the hard climb. With the singing wires to let General Howard know where they were, they had to keep moving. Only at night did they stop.

One night while they were camping at a place called Big Hole, a stirring in the camp awakened Running Bear. Somewhere nearby a horse nickered nervously. The next moment he heard stealthy footsteps; then the sharp crack of a rifle echoed through the sleeping camp, followed by cries of surprise from the people.

Running Bear got up quickly. He slung his medicine bundle over his shoulder and ran from his tent. It was near morning and in the gray dawn he glimpsed Joseph in the middle of the camp, issuing orders to his people.

"What is happening?" Running Bear asked.

142

"The bluecoats have found our camp," replied Joseph. "We must get the women, children, and old people on the trail at once."

"I will get the horses," Running Bear said.

By now everyone was running from the tepees, clutching what possessions they had. The men brought up the horses and travois and started the people moving again. The old ones and the children, slower to realize the danger, were shot down as they groped aimlessly about the camp. Running Bear heard the piercing cry of a four-year-old boy as a bullet went through his small leg. A squaw, carrying her baby in a shawl on her back, stumbled and sank to the ground with the blazing of a rifle nearby.

Running Bear choked back his rage and ran for a horse for Joseph's wife. Sarah was already mounted and being led from the camp.

Joseph's wife mounted the Apaloosa pony that Running Bear held for her, but suddenly she dropped down from her mount as if she had forgotten something. She was running back to the tepee when she stopped short, spun around, and sank to the ground.

Running Bear ran to her, with Joseph right behind him. But it was too late. A soldier's bullet had hit her, and she died in Joseph's arms.

Stunned with grief, Joseph carried his wife to his horse and galloped off with her lifeless body lying across the saddle. Running Bear scooped up the wounded boy in the curve of his arm and followed with the screaming child.

All along the trail women wailed the loss of their dead and children cried with fear. That night the dead were buried, Joseph's wife among them, and as the women still wailed and the children cried, Running Bear sat with his friend and shared his grief.

3

"THERE IS ONLY one way to keep ahead of General Howard," Joseph said several days after the surprise attack at Big Hole.

"And what way is that?" asked Looking Glass.

"We must stampede his horses," Joseph answered. "We will wait until nightfall, then a party of our young men will ride into the bluecoat camp and scatter the herd."

Ollicut volunteered to lead the stampede. With forty men he rode off into the dark prairie night. Joseph's plan worked. While the soldiers were busy rounding up their scattered horses, the Nez Percé bands were making their way into the Yellowstone country.

It was now early fall. The trees flamed yellow and gold, red and orange. The earth trembled before the spouting of geysers that sent plumes of water high into the air. Running

Bear's whole body trembled at the sight.

The Yellowstone was fine country, and it was good to stop and rest in peace. The hunters brought in game, and for the first time in many days the people had fresh meat to eat. The children played happily again, and their grandparents sat outside their tepees in the sun to regain their strength.

Then one day Little Runner reported that General Howard had gathered his horses and mules and was on the trail behind them. "We must leave this beautiful country," Joseph told his people. "We will go eastward on the old buffalo trails."

But they had no sooner started out when the singing wires betrayed them again. The lead scouts rode back to report that the way to the buffalo country was blocked by another troop of cavalrymen.

"What will we do?" Ollicut said bitterly. "The bluecoats have us blocked in both directions. We cannot go ahead and we cannot go back to the Yellowstone." He shook his head in disgust. "The bluecoats are everywhere. Is there no place in this great land where they cannot follow us?"

Suddenly Joseph looked at his brother and his eyes brightened. "Ollicut, you have just given me a thought. There *is* a place where the bluecoats cannot follow us."

"Where?" the chiefs asked in one voice. They moved closer to Joseph to hear the thought that Ollicut had given him.

Joseph said, "The way to the north is not blocked. If we cannot go to the buffalo country, we shall go to Canada. It is ruled by Grandmother England, and there is a Medicine Line, a boundary that separates it from the White Chief's country. No bluecoat will pursue us across the Medicine Line."

Old Too-hul-hul-sote frowned thoughtfully. "Will the

145

Grandmother take us in?" he asked. "Will the Canadian tribes welcome us?"

White Bird spoke up then. "I have heard that Sitting Bull and his Sioux were given refuge in Canada. The Sioux will give us shelter in their villages. They know how it is to be run off their lands by the bluecoats."

"Then it is settled," Joseph told his chiefs. "We will turn north to Canada."

They crossed the Yellowstone River and camped near Canyon Creek, but General Howard was fast on their trail. While Looking Glass and his band held off the bluecoats, Joseph got the people into Canyon Creek where he led them northward toward the Bear Paw Mountains. The days grew colder and the people were hungry, but with the bluecoats ever pursuing, they could not stop to hunt until they reached the protection of the mountains.

On and on they fled toward Canada. They crossed the Missouri River at Cow Island and when finally they reached the steep southern slopes of the Bear Paw Mountains, Joseph called a halt. The people were starving and exhausted and could not go on. They had to stop and rest.

"One more day's ride north and we will be in Canada," the chief called encouragement to the weary Nez Percés. "We will rest here and hunt; then we will be ready for the final journey."

"But what about the singing wires?" Running Bear reminded his friend when they were alone. "General Howard will soon find where our camp is."

For the first time Running Bear saw despair in Joseph's eyes. "Yes, the singing wires will carry his message to the soldiers here," the chief said. "Always there are more soldiers. They keep coming and coming. There is no end to them. They are everywhere."

"Then would it not be wiser to keep moving since we are so close to the Medicine Line?" Running Bear suggested.

Joseph nodded gravely. "It would be wiser, Running Bear, but in doing so more of the old and the sick would die. With rest and food they might live to see Canada. My duty is to protect *all* the people."

Running Bear nodded in understanding and rode up the trail to join the men who were cutting tent poles.

Soon lodges were made and the men had time to hunt. It was good to eat elk and buffalo meat again. The women cut up the meat and worked on the hides. Joseph's pretty daughter Sarah joined them with her scraper. She was fast becoming a woman, Running Bear thought, and Joseph was very proud of her.

When an icy wind from the north blew over the camp and somber gray clouds told that snow would soon be on the plains, Joseph knew it was time to travel. The Nez Percés gathered their robes and their meat and prepared for the last day's trek to Canada. Their spirits were high. Soon they would be in the Grandmother's Land where they could live in peace. Soon they would be with their friends the Sioux.

They broke camp early in the morning. While the women packed and tied the loads to the travois, the men went to the grazing grounds to herd the horses. White Bird and about two hundred people were mounted on their ponies, ready to leave.

They were just about to start out when the herd boys who were rounding up the last of the horses came riding into camp, shouting and waving their hands. It was then that Running Bear heard the blare of a bugle and the thunder of horses' hoofs pounding across the frozen plains.

Joseph shouted orders to White Bird and the men who rode guard for the departing people, urging them onward.

Digging their heels into the flanks of their mounts, White Bird's band started northward across the prairie as fast as they could go.

Running Bear leaped on a horse. He joined Joseph and the men in helping to rope the rest of the ponies. By now the soldiers were among the herd, trying to scatter them, but the Nez Percés were able to drive part of the herd behind the camp. It was there that Joseph found his frightened daughter, wandering aimlessly among the women.

Joseph caught her up and put her on a spotted Apaloosa pony. "Go with White Bird and those who have fled!" he told her.

Sarah was frightened. She didn't want to leave her father and tried to climb down from her horse. Joseph turned desperately to Running Bear.

"Go with her," he ordered. "Follow those who are already heading north."

"Are you coming, too?" Running Bear asked.

"No, I will stay here with the others and try to help them escape."

"But there will be no time," Running Bear protested. "The bluecoats are already at our camp."

"I cannot leave my people," Joseph said.

"Then I will stay with you," Running Bear answered.

"No," replied Joseph. "Those who run for the Grandmother's Land will need your help. The soldiers will soon be after them. Go, old friend!"

Before Running Bear could protest further, Joseph caught up the rope bridle of Sarah's horse and put it in his hand. The chief gave his daughter one last look, then slapped the two ponies on the rump and sent them galloping out of the camp.

With the open prairie ahead of them, Running Bear and

Sarah rode side by side in the direction of the fleeing band. A gale wind was in their faces and almost took their breath away.

"It will snow before nightfall," Running Bear called out to Sarah. But the girl didn't answer nor look up, and Running Bear knew that she was thinking about her father and the bluecoats back at the Bear Paw Mountains.

By the time they had caught up with the fleeing Nez Percés, the first flakes of snow began to fall. The little band kept on, plunging ahead through the whirling snow. Without shelter and the soldiers behind them, they had no other choice than to keep moving across the frozen plain.

Sarah rode in the center of the band with the women, and Running Bear fell back with the rear guard where he could keep a lookout for pursuing soldiers. Maybe the blizzard would keep them from following, he thought hopefully.

But his hopes were soon shattered when a shot rang out behind them and a young boy who was riding with the rear guard slumped over in his saddle. Running Bear took the boy up behind him, and as he did so he saw with horror the open, terror-filled eyes glazed with death. When the pursuing soldiers fell back, Running Bear laid the dead boy on the cold ground and covered him with his own blanket. There was nothing else to do.

The shadows of night came early on the stormy prairie, and they still hadn't reached the Grandmother's Land. White Bird kept urging them on. They would have to keep riding northward into the night until they crossed the Medicine Line. If they stopped, they would be captured by the soldiers.

Just before darkness closed in entirely, the bluecoats made a last desperate attack. Running Bear and the rear guard veered away from the band to head the soldiers off. Turning westward, they led the bluecoats into a coulee.

Bullets ricocheted against the rock walls as the soldiers charged after them. Running Bear urged his pony on, but the bluecoats were gaining on him. Ahead the other Nez Percés were searching desperately for cover behind the rocks.

Running Bear had just glimpsed a large boulder with a narrow trail behind it when a shot roared in his ears. The next instant his tough little Apaloosa pony trembled to the ground. As Running Bear made a dive for cover, a lead ball tore through his own flesh. He felt a sharp, stinging pain as if a firebrand had been thrust through his shoulder.

The next moment the earth seemed to crumble under him. The boulder went out of focus and swam above his head. The cries of soldiers and the sounds of galloping hoofs seemed a long way off. He sank to the cold ground and heard nothing more.

4

IT SEEMED as if he had been asleep for a long, long time—as if many moons had passed and he was in a different place, in a different time.

Running Bear opened his eyes and at first everything looked blurred. Then the face of a white man, staring down at him, came into focus. A stab of fear shot through Running Bear, and in a desperate attempt he tried to rise up. But pain and weakness made him drop back on the cot he was lying on. The white man put a hand on his arm. "Be quiet and rest," he said.

Running Bear studied the face warily. The man was younger than he. Perhaps he had seen twenty or more winters. His hair was cut short like a white man's and was the color of burnt copper. Out of the bearded face the eyes shone sharp and blue like turquoise.

The man made a sign of peace in the Indian sign language. He pointed to himself and then to Running Bear. "I am James Reed," he said, dragging each word out as if he were trying to make himself understood. "What is your name?"

Running Bear did not answer. His gaze drifted beyond the white man to the small cabin. A fire burned brightly on a stone hearth. In the center of the room was a rough table made of split logs. On it were piled open books and charts. The room reminded Running Bear of a soldier chief's cabin. Was he a captive of the bluecoats?

He struggled to sit up.

"Where—where am I?" he asked, and to his own ears his voice sounded like the creaking of bare branches in the wind.

The man smiled, and like most white men he used many words to answer a simple question. "I am glad you speak English because I know little of the Indian dialect," he said. "You are in my cabin. I built it last summer when I decided to stay here for a while to study the plants and animals in this region."

He pointed to the shadowy bunches of dried herbs and flowers hanging from beams across the ridgepole. "You see, I am a naturalist."

Running Bear didn't know what a naturalist was, nor did he care. At that moment he couldn't think of anything else than the sharp, painful twinge in his shoulder. He glanced down at the clean white bandage across it.

James Reed noticed this and explained, "It was lucky the bullet went through your shoulder and did not lodge in it. I am no surgeon and would not have liked to have dug it out. I made a paste from some of my healing herbs to put on the wound, and then I bandaged it."

At the mention of healing herbs, Running Bear thought of his own herbs in his medicine bundle. Where was the bundle now? he wondered. He knew he had it slung across his shoulder when his horse was shot from under him. He remembered grasping it as he sank to the ground with the bullet wound in his shoulder. It was the last thing he remembered doing.

He glanced anxiously around him. The white man seemed to have read his thoughts, for he pointed to the side of the cot. With relief Running Bear saw the medicine bundle on the floor, next to his moccasins.

As he stared at it everything that had happened came flooding back into his memory. The bluecoat attack, the fleeing band of Nez Percés, the blizzard, the pursuit in the coulee. But after that he couldn't remember a thing.

"How did I get here?" he asked the white man.

"I found you in the coulee behind a boulder," James Reed answered. "You must have been there all night in the blizzard because you were covered with snow. But there was a little life left in you, so I brought you to my cabin."

"Did my people get across the Medicine Line?" Running Bear asked eagerly.

James Reed nodded and smiled. "Your little band did. I heard it from a Sioux hunter. They are being cared for by Sitting Bull's people."

Running Bear pulled himself up painfully and looked at the man. "And the others?" he asked anxiously. "Was Joseph able to escape?"

The turquoise eyes fell, and the white man shook his head. "No, several days after your band left, Chief Joseph was captured in the Bear Paw Mountains by General Howard. He and the rest of your people have been sent to the reservation."

With a groan of anguish Running Bear lay back on the cot. All that long wandering—the struggle and the pain—for nothing! He turned his head toward the cabin wall. "How long have I been here?" he asked bitterly.

"You have been here about a week. You had a high fever from the bullet wound and from your exposure in the blizzard. I feared you wouldn't pull through until last night when the fever broke. Now today I know you will get well."

James Reed smiled with assurance at the sick man. "You are safe here with me," he said. "General Howard's army has left the Bear Paw Mountains, and when you are well, I will help you get to the Canadian border. It's not far from my cabin."

The fever had left Running Bear so weak that he could barely sit up. During the day while James Reed was out searching the coulee and prairie for specimens of rare plants, Running Bear rested and dozed in the cabin. At night the naturalist sat by his cot and talked. He told Running Bear that all the snow had melted from the prairie, but the tops of the mountains still wore a white mantle.

Every night James Reed read by the fireside from a large black book. One night Running Bear's curiosity got the better of him and he asked, "What is that book you are reading?"

"It is the White Man's Good Book," James answered. "Would you like me to read from it aloud?"

Running Bear nodded, and James began to read from the Bible. The words brought the wounded Nez Percé great comfort, and every night he asked James to read to him.

' One night after James had been reading from the Gospels, Running Bear said in a puzzled voice, "Your Great Spirit Chief says that man should love his neighbor as

154

himself, and that is good. But the White Man does not live the way the good son in your Bible tells him to live. Why does the White Man not do what his Great Spirit Chief says?"

James closed the Bible, and his blue eyes were hooded with sadness. "I do not know, Running Bear. The world would be a much better place to live in if he did."

Trust and friendship grew between the two men, and when Running Bear was able to move about the cabin, he opened his medicine bundle to show his friend his most precious possessions. James was surprised to see a white man's coin among the herbs, roots, and buffalo stones. Then Running Bear told him how a white girl named Nancee had given him the amulet when he had freed her from the Blackfoot camp.

James took a great interest in the old coin. He turned it over in his hand to study it. "It is very old," he observed. "I daresay it was one of the first cent pieces minted by the United States government."

"Nancee called it her good luck penny," Running Bear explained. He paused a moment, then looked at the white man. "It brought me good medicine when you found me in the coulee."

James smiled and handed the coin back to Running Bear. "It seems as if this penny was meant to bring good fortune," he agreed.

Running Bear placed the coin carefully inside his medicine bundle. "Tomorrow," he said as he closed the bundle, "I must leave you, James Reed. I am well now, and I must find my people in Canada."

James looked down at his empty hands for a long moment. He would miss Running Bear. "I shall be unhappy to see you go," he murmured.

Running Bear nodded soberly. "You are my friend and I, too, am unhappy to leave, but it is time I be with my people. They will need my help in a strange land."

James Reed looked at his friend and nodded in understanding.

5

A BRIGHT SUN shone down on the two men as they rode up the trail together on James Reed's big brown horse. The sun threw long shadows across their way and warmed the resinous pines so that they scented the crisp autumn air. Running Bear drew in deeply the scented air and felt alive and whole again.

When the trail narrowed into the coulee, James Reed dismounted and led the horse by its bridle.

"I can walk, too," Running Bear protested.

But James shook his head. "It is your first day out and it is better that you ride, Running Bear. Anyway, I am used to walking this trail when I search for my plants."

They came out of the coulee to rolling plains that sloped gently away to the northeast. Riding together now, James coaxed his horse to a brisk trot. As they were crossing a rise,

Running Bear glanced back at the Bear Paw Mountains and thought of Joseph, the calm and wise one—the man of peace.

Far to the south lay the Yellowstone, Big Hole, and the Lolo Trail, and to the westward was the beautiful Land of the Winding Waters where the bones of his ancestors lay. A vision of the proud Nez Percé chiefs astride their painted ponies rose before Running Bear's eyes. He would keep that vision with him always, even though his tribe was scattered and beaten.

He turned his eyes to the north and raised his head high. He would find Sarah and the people who had escaped to the Grandmother's Land. He would be with them in their pain and their sorrows, just as Joseph would have wanted him to be.

Not far from the coulee they reached the Medicine Line. James Reed pulled the horse to a halt and dismounted. He pointed ahead to a grove of golden aspen trees. "That is Canada," he said. "The trail crosses the border here and leads to a small French Canadian settlement. The people there are good and will give you food and shelter. They will tell you how to find the Sioux and your people."

Running Bear was about to dismount, but James handed him the reins. "The horse is yours, Running Bear. You will need it in your search for your people. I can get another horse at the trading post."

Running Bear looked at his friend with gratitude. What could he give in return? he wondered. All that he had was in his medicine bundle. The herbs, the roots, the buffalo stones did not seem enough to give to a man who had saved his life.

Then he thought of a grateful girl who had nothing to give, either, except her good luck penny. Thinking of that

158

long-ago night, he opened his medicine bundle, and his fingers curled around the small leather pouch. Slowly he drew out his amulet. He took James Reed's hand and put the copper coin into it.

James looked down at the old penny with surprise. The sun struck it, and it shone like burnished gold—like the aspen leaves in the grove across the Medicine Line.

"But it is your amulet!" he protested.

Running Bear nodded. "It was my amulet. Now it is yours. May it bring my white brother good medicine."

They clasped hands solemnly; then Running Bear touched the horse, reined it around, and rode toward the aspens. Before he disappeared through the trees, he turned and waved farewell. James Reed waved back and watched until the trees hid the Nez Percé from sight.

"May God grant you a safe journey," he called after his Indian friend. Then squeezing the good luck penny in his fist, he turned back along the trail in the direction of his lonely cabin.

VINH

1

JON REED felt as though he were being aroused from a long sleep. A hand shook his shoulder gently.

"Hi, Jon. How are you feeling?" The voice sounded vaguely familiar.

"I think he's coming around now," said the voice again.

Jon opened his eyes and blinked them until the blurred faces came into focus. His dad and mom were smiling down at him, and between them stood Miss Karcher.

"How are you feeling?" the nurse asked again.

"Okay—I guess," Jon answered in a voice that didn't quite sound like his own.

"It's all over now, son," Mr. Reed told him, beaming. "Soon you'll be on your feet and walking around like the rest of us. Dr. Bannon said that the operation was a success."

Jon looked up at his father. "Really, Dad?"

His father nodded, and Jon smiled his first real big smile in a long time. Then his gaze flew down to his leg which was incased in a white cast from his ankle to his hip. "How long will my leg be in this cast?"

"For quite a while, Jon," Miss Karcher replied. "But each day it will be healing and getting stronger."

His mother reached over and squeezed his hand. "We prayed that the operation would be a success, Jon," she said, her lips trembling, "and God answered our prayers. We are so grateful."

"And you've been a very brave boy, son," his father added proudly.

Jon turned his eyes away from his parents and glanced down at his cast again. "I wasn't so brave last night before the operation," he confessed. "If it weren't for that good luck penny you gave me, Dad, I'd have been really scared." He looked around his bed and over at the nightstand. "Hey, where is my penny?"

Miss Karcher opened the drawer to the nightstand. "I put it back in its box to keep it safe for you, Jon."

"Can I have it now?"

"Of course you can," Miss Karcher said, taking the coin out of its small box and handing it to him.

Jon looked down at the old penny and traced the Liberty head with his finger. His lips spread out into a happy smile as he closed his hand around the coin. His eyes drooped shut. He felt tired . . . so tired. Still holding his good luck penny, he drifted off to sleep again.

The days passed slowly. Jon read all the books his parents brought him and watched so much TV that he was sick of it. He wished he could get out of this room. He was tired of staring at the four narrow walls.

Then one day Dr. Bannon said that Jon was strong enough to sit in a wheelchair, and Miss Karcher wheeled one in with a special lift for his cast to rest on. The nurse helped Jon wheel himself out of his room and into the solarium at the far end of the hall. She showed him how to push the big wheels with his hands and how to operate the little brake to stop and hold the wheels.

Soon Jon was able to wheel himself almost everywhere. It was fun to scoot up and down the hall in his wheelchair and get to know the other kids in the hospital.

He guessed he had showed his Liberty Cap penny to almost every kid in the children's wing. There was a boy who took a special interest in it and wanted to swap his new model airplane for the penny. But Jon shook his head and said it was his good luck penny and he wanted to keep it.

One afternoon when Jon wheeled himself into the solarium, he saw a boy he hadn't seen before. He was a small, frail boy with golden skin and long black hair. He was looking out of the window, his dark eyes empty of any expression.

"Hi," Jon said cheerfully as he wheeled his chair beside the new boy. The boy didn't answer but kept staring out the window.

When Jon asked Miss Karcher about this strange, quiet boy, the nurse said that he was a Vietnamese refugee who had just come to this country. "His name is Vinh," Miss Karcher said, as she straightened Jon's bed, smoothing the sheets and fluffing the pillow.

"Why does he just sit there and stare out the window?" Jon wanted to know. "He didn't even answer me when I said hi to him. Doesn't he know how to speak English?"

"Oh, he knows a little English," Miss Karcher said. "His foster father told us they're teaching Vinh how to speak it."

165

"Then why didn't he answer me when I said hi?" Jon asked with a puzzled frown. "He ought to know what hi means."

"Well, I guess it's because everything is so strange to him here," Miss Karcher replied. "He hasn't been in this country very long. What he needs is a friend—a friend like you, Jon."

"What's wrong with him?" asked Jon. "I mean, why is he here in the hospital?"

"Vinh has been through a lot, including malnutrition," Miss Karcher said. "He's here for a complete physical. We hope to build him up so that he can be a healthy boy like you."

"What's mal—nutrition?" Jon asked.

Miss Karcher laughed. "That's one thing you won't have to worry about, Jon, by the way you wolf down your meals." Her face grew serious. "Malnutrition means that Vinh hadn't gotten enough to eat in Vietnam. The effects of malnutrition take a long time to cure."

"Boy," Jon replied, frowning, "it must be terrible not to get enough to eat."

"It surely is," Miss Karcher said.

Jon let out a big sigh and glanced ruefully at his cast. "Well, at least Vinh can walk."

Miss Karcher gave the bed a final pat and turned to him with a smile. "You'll be walking soon, too," she said. "Dr. Bannon told me you'll be going home at the end of the week."

"No kidding!" Jon yelled, almost jumping out of his wheelchair for joy.

Miss Karcher made a mock frown. "Don't you like us here?"

"Oh—no! I don't mean that," Jon added hastily. "You're

166

swell, Miss Karcher, and so is everyone else. It's just that—I mean—"

Miss Karcher smiled again. "I know what you mean, Jon."

When she left the room, Jon thought about what she had said—about going home. It seemed so long since he had been home. He thought about sleeping in his own room again with its familiar bed and furniture. He thought about his coin collection that his father had mounted for him and had hung on his wall. He thought about his dog, Toby, who liked to sleep under his bed at night to keep him company. All these familiar things were so dear to him that he couldn't imagine what it would be like not to have them to return to.

And then he thought about Vinh, alone in a strange country.

He swung his wheelchair around and rolled it out of his room and down the hall to the solarium. Vinh was still sitting alone by the window, staring out at nothing. It was as if he hadn't moved an inch since Jon had left him.

Jon rolled his chair up to the boy and sat quietly by his side. Miss Karcher had said that what Vinh needed was a friend. But what could he say to this strange, silent boy?

Then Jon remembered how interested all the other kids were in his old penny. He slipped his hand into his shirt pocket and brought out the box holding his Liberty Cap cent. He opened the box and held the penny out for Vinh to see. The Vietnamese boy turned his head and looked at the coin; then he turned away again.

Jon nudged the boy and pointed to the 1794 date. "Old penny," he said slowly, hoping Vinh would understand. "Very old penny. One of first coins minted in this country. Do you like old coins?"

Vinh gave him a blank stare and made no answer. He was

167

about to turn to the window again when Jon pointed to the letters above the Liberty head. "That word means freedom, he told Vinh. "You know, free—dom."

At the sound of the word, the Vietnamese boy glanced back at Jon, and then down at the coin where Jon's finger curved around the word Liberty. There seemed to be a flicker of recognition in the sad, dark eyes. For a long moment Vinh sat there, staring at the letters around the top of the coin.

2

THAT NIGHT, just before visiting hours were over, a strange man and woman stepped into Jon's room. At first Jon thought they had made a mistake and had come to the wrong room. But they walked right up to Jon's bed and stood smiling down at him. Jon couldn't help smiling back because they looked so friendly.

"Are you Jon Reed?" the man asked.

Jon nodded.

"Well, we are Mr. and Mrs. Nowicki," the man said. "We are Vinh's foster parents."

Jon sat up in bed and studied his visitors with interest. Mr. Nowicki was tall and his shoulders were slightly stooped. He had a boyish-looking face with a lock of unruly brown hair falling across his forehead. Mrs. Nowicki was small and blond, with gentle blue eyes.

169

"You see, Vinh has been with us for only a week," Mr. Nowicki explained. "He is one of the Vietnamese refugees our church has sponsored."

"He has been through so much," Mrs. Nowicki put in, her blue eyes sad. "He lost both his parents in South Vietnam and had no home. He was found wandering around the streets with other homeless children. They are called street children because that's the only place they have to live, and they have to beg for what little food they get to eat."

Mr. Nowicki moved closer to Jon's bed. "To Vinh the world is a cruel and lonely place," he added, "but we're trying to change all that."

"Miss Karcher told us that you had tried to make friends with him this afternoon, Jon," Mrs. Nowicki said with a warm smile, "and Vinh told us about a coin you showed him that had the word freedom on it. He knows what that word means. It's one of the few American words that he understands."

Mr. Nowicki reached out to squeeze Jon's hand. "Anyway, Vinh has taken quite an interest in you and your coin, Jon," he said. "And we want to thank you for being his friend today."

Jon blushed and looked down at his hands. "Oh, that's okay." Then he asked, "When Vinh gets out of the hospital, will he be going to school?"

"Oh, yes," Mrs. Nowicki said. "He'll be going to Clearview School, here in the city."

"Clearview!" exclaimed Jon. "That's where I go. Boy, we have a neat baseball team. I hope I can play this spring. The guys said they'd let me join the team when I can walk."

"So you like baseball," Mr. Nowicki mused, his eyes twinkling. "So do I, and I hope Vinh will like it too."

Miss Karcher rustled into the room at that moment to announce that visiting hours were over. Mr. and Mrs. Nowicki said good-bye and thanked Jon again for talking to Vinh that afternoon.

After the Nowickis left, Miss Karcher looked down at Jon with a twinkle. "Well," she said, tucking the sheet around him and fluffing his pillow for the night, "Didn't I say what that boy needed was a friend like you, Jon?"

On Friday morning Jon's mother came to take him home. Dr. Bannon came into the room with her to give Jon last-minute instructions.

"You'll have to put up with that cast a few weeks longer, Jon," he said. "And when the cast comes off, you'll have to report back here every day for a while for therapy. But by spring you should be walking around just fine."

"Good enough to play baseball?" asked Jon eagerly.

"Good enough for that," Dr. Bannon answered with a grin. He reached over the bed to shake hands with Jon, then left the room.

Miss Karcher helped Mrs. Reed pack Jon's clothes and books. "Now you're all ready to check out, Jon," she said. "Let's get you into your wheelchair."

"But I can walk with crutches now," Jon protested.

"Hospital regulations," Miss Karcher told him. "All patients get wheeled out."

She helped Jon into the wheelchair and was about to push him down the hall when Jon said, "I'd like to say good-bye to Vinh, Miss Karcher. You and Mom wait here and I'll be right back."

He wheeled himself up the hall to Vinh's room. Vinh was sitting up in bed, watching TV. His eyes brightened when he saw Jon.

171

"I'm going home," Jon said as he wheeled his chair up to Vinh's bed.

Vinh nodded that he understood, then turned to watch the TV show. It was some dumb game show, Jon noticed, and Vinh probably didn't understand a thing that was going on. He was just watching it for something to do.

"I hear you'll be going to Clearview School," Jon broke in. "That's where I go to school."

Vinh glanced back at Jon.

"Hey, maybe we can both be on the baseball team," Jon said. "You know—baseball?"

"Base—ball?" asked Vinh, puzzled.

"Yeah, baseball," Jon repeated, imitating a batter batting a ball.

"I—no know how," Vinh said.

"I never played either," Jon told him, "but we can learn together."

For a long moment both boys sat silently looking at one another. Then Jon thrust his hand in his shirt pocket, and his fingers touched the little box that held his good luck penny.

The old penny had been in the family for three generations, Dad had said, but now it belonged to Jon to do with as he pleased. He would miss his good luck penny, even though he had had it for only a short time. But he had the feeling that the penny was meant to be passed on, just as the Nez Percé had passed it on to his great-great-grandfather. Anyway, he guessed that Vinh needed it now more than he.

Slowly he drew the coin from its box. He reached out for Vinh's narrow hand and put the penny into it. "Here, Vinh, you can have my good luck penny," he said.

Vinh stared at the penny in his hand. He traced the word Liberty with his thin finger. "Free—dom," he murmured.

"Yeah, it means freedom," Jon replied.

"Free—dom. Is good." Vinh looked up at Jon and his dark eyes were shining. He bowed the low, gracious Vietnamese bow and said, "Thank you, Jon."

Jon glanced down at his empty hands. "Well, I'll see you around," he said as he turned his chair toward the door. But before he left the room, he glanced back at Vinh who was still looking at the coin. For the first time Jon saw a quiet smile spread across the frail, pinched face, and then he knew for sure that Vinh needed the penny more than he.

Like Captain Jeremy Roberts, almost two centuries before him, Jon Reed moved slowly away from his good luck penny. His hand would feel empty without the familiar copper coin to hold, but for some strange reason his heart was much lighter. Perhaps it was because the good luck penny—like happiness—was meant to be passed on.

Jon rolled his chair down the hallway, and by the time he reached his mother and Miss Karcher he was whistling a happy tune.

Ruth Nulton Moore lives in Bethlehem, Pennsylvania, with her husband who is a professor of accounting at Lehigh University. They have two grown sons and a granddaughter.

Specializing in English literature, she received a BA from Bucknell University and an MA from Columbia University. She did postgraduate work in education at the University of Pittsburgh.

A former schoolteacher, Mrs. Moore has written for *Children's Activities* and *Jack and Jill*. She is the author of eleven published novels for children, among them, *Ghost Bird Mystery* and *Danger in the Pines*, both published by Herald Press. Her books sell in England, Sweden, Finland, and Puerto Rico as well as in the United States and Canada.

Mrs. Moore is a member of Children's Authors and Illustrators of Philadelphia, and her biography appears in *Contemporary Authors, The International Authors and Writers Who's Who,* and the *Dictionary of International Biography* and *Pennsylvania Women in History.* When she is not at her typewriter, she is busy lecturing about her art of writing to students in the public schools and colleges in her area. She also teaches Sunday school at Christ Church, United Church of Christ in Bethlehem.